Also in the Hippo Adventure series:

Attack of the Vampirates
Revenge of the Vampirates
Martin Oliver

Look out for:
Strange Hiding Place 2: SYSTEM CRASH
Strange Hiding Place 3: DOWNLOAD
Graham Marks

Hippo Adventure

STRANGE HIDING PLACE 1
HARD DRIVE

Graham Marks

Hippo

Scholastic Children's Books
7–9 Pratt Street, London NW1 0AE, UK
a division of Scholastic Publications Ltd
London ~ New York ~ Toronto ~ Sydney ~ Auckland

First published by Scholastic Publications Ltd, 1995

ISBN 0 590 13105 2

All rights reserved
Typeset by TW Typesetting, Midsomer Norton, Avon
Printed by Cox & Wyman Ltd, Reading, Berks.

10 9 8 7 6 5 4 3 2 1

To Leo

Chapter 1

Whispers in the air. Scrambled messages on an unknown frequency. Invisible commands to silent watchers...

"Scanners tracking the southern quadrant have a pick-up. Do you read?" they said.

"Reading," came the reply.

"Confirm distance."

"Two kliks and closing."

"Units in place?"

"Yes."

"All systems operational?"

"All systems operational."

"Estimate time to final countdown."

"Four minutes. The accident is waiting to happen."

*　*　*

It had been a long day and Dez was getting fed up. He was stuck in the back of the car, watching countryside that his mother kept describing as "wonderful" but which he was thoroughly sick of.

His father was fed up as well. Fed up with Dez for getting himself lost in the little town they'd stopped at for lunch. Their timetable was now, according to his dad, shot to pieces – though why they had to have a timetable at all Dez couldn't understand. They were on holiday, driving around somewhere in France called the Dordogne (which sounded to Dez more like a medical condition than a place), and timetables were for school – somewhere he wouldn't be for at least another six weeks.

"Dammit, Mary – it'll be dark in half an hour!" Dez sank further down in the back seat so he couldn't be seen in the rear-view mirror.

"That doesn't mean you have to drive like Damon Hill, Ted." His mother had never cottoned on to the fact that Dad liked having his driving criticized even less than he liked being late.

As his parents squabbled in the front, Dez picked up his Game Boy and, with the sound turned down ("Switch that off, please – I can't concentrate with all that mindless beeping. We *are* driving on the wrong side of the road, you know!"), he let his mind wander. When they got back to England it would be to a new house and the slightly worrying prospect of a new school.

New school, new teachers, new boys – friends or enemies, who could tell? – and only his dog, Rufus, to help him through the inevitable bad times. Dez was a natural optimist, always thinking the best, but he knew that the first few weeks of September were going to be tough. He was determined to enjoy this holiday, timetable or no timetable, even if it was supposed to help him with his French.

He looked up from the tiny glowing screen

in his lap. It really was getting dark now. The car's headlights, with those funny bits of black tape stuck on them, were lighting up the road ahead, but it twisted and turned so much you couldn't see a lot. Maybe it was the dark, but he thought his mum could be right – they did seem to be going quite fast.

On the side of the road nearest the car the jagged silhouettes of fir trees made an almost impenetrable wall as they zipped by; on the opposite side low, scraggy bushes led off to yet more trees. It had been like that for the past half hour. At this rate, surely they'd be at their hotel soon.

He had just gone back to blasting alien blips to pixels when he heard his mother gasp. He sat up straight, undid his seat-belt and moved over to her side of the car.

"Ted!" she shouted, pointing at the approaching bend in the road. "Ted – slow down!"

Dez could just make out the dark shape his mother had spotted first because she was sitting where the driver should be. It looked like a brick wall, and the thought flashed through his mind that it must be a broken-down lorry.

"The brakes aren't working!"

Dez looked at his father, mouth open, face lit up by the soft green light of the dashboard. His arms were rigid in front of him, as if he was trying to force himself through his seat and into the back of the car.

"We're going faster!"

Right then time seemed to slow, stretch, e-x-p-a-n-d.

Dez watched, fascinated, as the huge black shape in the road grew even bigger. He watched his father fight with the steering wheel and gear stick, almost as if they were attacking him. He watched his mother twist slowly round to look at him, her left hand reaching between the seats, the diamonds in her engagement ring glinting. The last thing he remembered doing was flicking up the lock on his door.

Chapter 2

Dez woke up.

Had he been dreaming? He opened his eyes and made out a strange orange light somewhere in front of him. He was lying on his side, and everything he owned seemed to ache as he moved his left hand down to help push himself up. If he was in bed it was a bed covered in dust and small stones... Then it all came tumbling back. Their car had crashed! The orange light was fire – his parents could still be trapped!

Dez tried to stand, his feet scrabbling in the dirt. Suddenly he felt a hand on his shoulder, pushing him gently down and pulling him back at the same time. He froze. And then he heard a man's voice.

"Stay still," it whispered. "You are in great danger – move away from the road."

There was something odd about the way the man spoke, but his voice had an edge that made Dez do what he said. He glanced over his shoulder to look at the speaker as he squirmed further back under the spiky bushes. For a moment all he could see was a dark shape, but then the light from the road intensified and he could make out the man's face and the fact that he was wearing what appeared to be black mechanic's overalls.

With the burst of light Dez remembered the car. It was burning! He couldn't just lie there if his parents were inside, injured and unable to get out. Breaking free from the man's grip, Dez lurched forward, only to be thrown back, punched by the force of a huge explosion.

For a moment the night sky was lit up by a vivid gout of flame that reached up five, ten metres and then slowly sank down. Dez's ears felt as if someone had boxed them and his head seemed to be looser than it should be on his shoulders. Gasping for breath he peered through the tangle of bushes towards the burning car and was stunned to see what appeared to be men in uniform gathering round it for a second or two. One then gave an order, gesturing with a gun, and they ran off.

The night was strangely silent after the dragon's roar of the explosion, and then in the silence Dez could hear a high-pitched whine in his ears, like you do after a big bang. He felt something wet on his face and realized that he was crying.

"There's nothing we can do," said the man's voice. Dez had forgotten all about him and whirled round in a panic. Crouched right next to him, the stranger's face had an odd, wax-like quality, shadows waving across it as he spoke.

"We have to get away from here," he went on. "Follow me – and be as quiet as you can."

"But my parents…" said Dez, looking back at the road.

"All I can tell you is that it was very quick," said the man, indicating that Dez should follow him through the bushes and away from the road.

"Who were those men? What happened?"

"I can't go into details now." The man held a thorny branch back to let Dez through a small gap, and, too confused to do anything else, he followed.

When they reached the trees and were able to stand up, Dez was about to speak when he heard a soft sucking noise in the distance. The man stopped and looked at a small box in his hand. He smiled slightly.

"They've gone," he muttered and began walking away from the road again, deeper into the forest.

"Who?" asked Dez, running to keep up with him and stumbling in the dark. "Who's gone? Where are you taking me? Shouldn't we call the police … are *you* the police?"

"I will explain everything – as far as I can – when we get to where we're going," came the reply. "For the moment you just have to trust me."

Trust. Small word, big responsibility. But for Dez there was no choice. Even though he'd been warned, ever since he could re- member, not to go off with strangers, what choice did he have? Either stay where he was, stranded by the side of a French road in the gathering dark, or go with this man. Dez mentally flipped a coin, stood looking at the man looking at him, and then nodded.

"OK," he said, wondering as he followed if he'd done the right thing.

Their journey was a short one. There wasn't exactly a path through the trees, and there was no light to see where they were going, but the man led the way without once bumping into anything and Dez followed his black- against-black shape like a puppy.

As he walked, his mind was in a turmoil.

His parents were dead. Well, not his *real* parents – he was an adopted child – but they were the only parents he had. For all he knew his real parents could be dead as well, and it occurred to him that for this sort of thing to happen to a person twice in eleven years was totally unfair.

He'd been in foster homes until he was five and counted himself lucky to have been adopted at all. People only seemed to want babies, little squirts they could pretend were their own, and when Ted and Mary Danby had come into his life it was like ten Christmases arriving at once. And now they were gone. In a way Dez was used to it; people had been going from his life all of his life, though usually it was in a far less dramatic way.

He was alone again, and he was going to have to get used to the idea.

A few minutes after leaving the roadside the man stopped in a clearing and Dez almost bumped into him.

"What's happened?" he asked, peering round the man. There was nothing to see.

"We're here."

"Where?" said Dez, walking past the man and into the clearing.

"Careful."

"Why? There's nothing he— *Oof!*" It felt as if he'd walked straight into a tree, but when he stumbled back and looked, there was nothing there.

"I told you to be careful," said the man. He pointed his fist in Dez's direction and the thing in his hand clicked. Dez heard the sort of sound a TV screen makes when you turn it on and the air in front of him flickered. One moment there was nothing and the next he was staring at a sleek, ultra-modern van.

"How…?" Dez put his hand out and touched the vehicle with the tips of his fingers. It was real, it was solid, it was there.

"Intra-molecule expansion," the man said, smiling as he walked forward, clicking the thing in his hand again and making a door appear in the side of the van. It hissed as it opened.

"What?"

"That's how we do it," the man said, pulling the door open and waving at Dez to follow him inside. "It's called 'cloaking'."

Dez stood stock still and looked at the man, half of him lit by the yellow interior light of the van, his shadow cast on the leafy ground. Feelings crowded in on him like spectators at an accident, all wanting to be in front – amazement, fear and loss, all covered in the cold blanket of shock.

What was he doing here in this chilly French wood, alone with a stranger? Shouldn't he have waited by the car for the police to come? Why did he believe a word this man said? He could be anyone. What on earth, thought Dez, had made him think he'd be safer going with him? From inside the van he heard what sounded like a soft chirruping. *Budgies?*

All this time the man had watched him, saying nothing, staying still. Then, ignoring the weird birdcalls, he moved towards him and put his hand on Dez's shoulder and patted it, just like his dad used to do. The simple gesture made Dez feel a lot calmer, more at ease, and he knew, just somehow *knew*, that everything would be all right if he got in the van. He walked slowly to the door, hesitated, and then got in, the man following him. There was another sighing hiss of air as the door swung shut.

More whispers. More questions.

"*Success?*" they asked.

"As far as we can tell," they answered.

"*What?*"

"There was an explosion."

"*Why?*"

"The machine they were in was far cruder than we imagined, little more than a travelling bomb. But, as far as we can tell, we succeeded."

"*I hope so. Stay for another circuit or so, just to check. We will be in touch.*"

Chapter 3

While the outside of the van had un-
doubtedly looked very modern, very
streamlined, the inside was something else
entirely. It didn't look to Dez as if there was
any way these four wheels could have rolled
off a production line *anywhere* on Earth. But
if they hadn't, where had they come from? A
Hollywood special effects studio? His eyes
almost out on stalks, he sank into a chair and
refused to follow that particular chain of
thought, it was too confusing.

The seat he was sitting on moulded itself to
his body the moment he sat down. It was the
oddest sensation and he felt as if he was

suspended in mid-air, being gently massaged – which was just what he needed after being flung out of a speeding car and across a road. He didn't seem to have broken anything, but he did ache quite a lot.

Then there was the smell (sort of moth-bally, but nicer) and the fact that he was surrounded by the most mind-boggling display of equipment he'd ever seen.

The van was divided into two compart-ments, the bit he and the man were sitting in and, through a small gap, the actual driving bit. Dez stared, mouth open, at large, flat screens. Some danced with weird hiero-glyphics, others projected three-dimensional pictures – aerial views of wooded countryside, what looked like the solar system and other things he couldn't make out – and yet others showed objects that moved and gave the distinct impression that they were, in some odd way, *thinking*.

And all the time, in the background, he could hear strange bird-like squawking, cheeping noises. Was someone talking?

The more he looked, the more convinced he became that there was nothing twentieth-century about the van, nothing at all. But (and this was what he was still finding hardest to think about) if it wasn't twentieth-century technology, what was it? In books people pinched themselves when they thought they might be dreaming, but Dez had already woken up once to find that everything around him was real. Pinching himself would only be a painful waste of time.

He turned to look at the man. Somehow he looked more real here than he had out by the road. His skin had lost its waxy appearance, and it occurred to Dez, looking down at his dust-covered, scuffed clothes, that *he* probably looked quite odd himself.

"Maybe I should try and explain a few things, Jack," said the man. Dez looked at him and frowned. "Are you feeling all right?"

"Yes ... but, you know ... how did you know my name was Jack?" Nobody called

Dez "Jack" any more, not since primary school, not even his parents. His surname was Danby, and someone, he couldn't remember who, had nicknamed him "Desperate". He'd been Desperate Danby for a month or two, and simply Dez from then on. It was strange to be called Jack after so long, but then everything was strange at the moment.

"I know rather more than just your name, Jack." The man reached over to a console that looked like a kitchen work surface covered in blisters, tapped it and said something Dez couldn't understand. The screen cleared and then threw up yet more of the dancing hieroglyphics; they twisted and squirmed like coloured worms, wriggling across the thin grey sliver of ... what? Plastic? Metal? He couldn't tell.

"Well, you don't know that no one calls me Jack." Dez sat forward, and the back of the chair moved with him. "And anyway, what's *your* name?"

"How rude of me," replied the man,

looking slightly surprised. "My name is Yakob. So, if you aren't called Jack, what *are* you called?"

"Dez," said Dez, watching as the man called Yakob tapped the console again. The worms tangoed. "Everyone calls me Dez."

"I shall as well."

"You were going to explain things to me." Dez rubbed some dirt off his face as he spoke. "What happened out there?" He took a deep breath, swallowed the lump that had suddenly appeared in his throat and pointed back to the road, "Why are my, um ... why are my *parents* dead? And what were *you* doing there?"

"I was sent to rescue you, Jack – sorry, Dez." Yakob leaned back in his chair. "I came a long way to make sure you would be safe, and, to be honest, I arrived too late."

"But I *am* safe, aren't I?"

"More by luck than anything to do with me," said Yakob.

"What do you mean?"

"Somehow or other you were thrown out of your car." Yakob fiddled with the small matchbox-sized thing in his hand. "The Väd-Raatch meant you to die in that crash, and it was pure chance that you didn't. None of this," his hand swept round the weird clutter of humming, seemingly alive stuff that surrounded them both, "could have stopped it from happening."

"Why would they want to kill *me*? What have *I* ever done to them? And anyway, who are they? What did you call them? The Väd-wotsits?" Dez could feel things welling up inside him once more – things he couldn't control, like tears and stuff. He wanted to cry, but he couldn't quite remember how. Actually, what he *really* wanted to do was kick something very hard.

He was alive, but his parents weren't. He was alone in the world. No brothers, no sisters, no grandparents – just some sister of his father's, somewhere in Australia, who no one had heard from for years. And he was in the middle of the French countryside, a long way from home. Then he remembered they were moving house soon, and didn't really have a home at the moment. *Total* bummer.

Yakob looked at Dez in the kind of way people do when they don't quite know what to say, and took a deep breath. "You'll have to listen to what my Wing Leader, Tor Kobal, has to tell you for the full story," he said at last, reaching behind him and picking up a small silver oblong. "But before I play you this, I have to tell you something you may find very hard to believe."

"Harder to believe than some people I've never heard of trying to kill me?" interrupted Dez.

"Quite possibly."

"Tell me, then."

But before Yakob could say anything something in the van screeched out loudly and all the lights dimmed.

"What's happening?" gasped Dez.

"Scoutship overflight ... low and slow,"

Yakob said, then turned and spoke again, but this time in what Dez assumed was his own language. Seconds later every screen in the van blanked and there was complete silence. No one spoke, no one moved. In the yellow half-light Dez sat rigid in his chair, wondering what the heck was going on. He didn't dare say or do anything and as the seconds ticked by all he could do was try to stop his teeth from chattering. He wasn't cold, so he knew he must be frightened. The unknown is very good at doing that.

Then one of the holo-screens lit up next to Yakob, information of some sort streaming across it at a rate of knots.

"Right overhead…" Yakob muttered to himself, and Dez couldn't help looking up; somewhere above the roof a hunter stalked. "Why aren't they going? They can't have picked anything up – there! Moving away…"

"Can we, um … can we talk?" whispered Dez.

"We can."

"What's a scoutship overflight?"

"The Väd–Raatch are checking the area," explained Yakob. "Being typically thorough."

"Can they see us? Will they be able to find us?"

"They're not looking for us, and they don't know we're here," said Yakob, studying the screen. "And if you don't know what you're looking for, you very rarely find it."

"So why all the precautions?" asked Dez.

"Because if they *did* happen to pick us up we'd be in real trouble."

"I thought I was in real trouble already," sighed Dez.

"This would be real trouble and a half," said Yakob, sitting back. "Good, they're out of range ... for the moment."

"For the moment?"

Yakob turned and said something over his shoulder to whoever or whatever it was in the van he spoke to, and the lights brightened. "They may come back," he said, "or they may not. What were we doing before all that?"

"You were going to tell me something you said I'd find hard to believe," said Dez.

"Right, so I was. All right. I've already told you my name is Yakob, Yakob Pell. What I didn't say was that I am a Tylurian from Priam IV, a planet somewhere behind what I'm told you call the Cygnus Rift – that's in the Orion Arm of the Milky Way, 300,000 light years from here – give or take a light year." Yakob pointed to himself. "I am – how would you put it? – an alien."

"You don't *look* like one," Dez said, peering at Yakob, staring in a way he'd been told he never should. "You look just like one of us."

"Appearances can be deceptive."

"Huh?" frowned Dez.

"Don't judge people by what they look like – they aren't always what they seem," explained Yakob, reaching over and placing the silver thing on the console. There was a hiss, like the sound of a bottle of fizzy water opening, as it changed colour and somehow became part of the surface. "I'm going to play the holo now, so listen carefully."

He waited for a second or two and then a dark circle next to Dez crackled and lit up. A cylinder of light, about a metre high, shot up out of it and started to change shape. Then, quite suddenly, Dez was gaping at the figure of a woman dressed in some kind of uniform. She looked like a very expensive plastic kit he'd seen in a comic shop once, and then she moved, waving her arm.

"That's a holo of my Wing Leader, Tor Kobal," said Yakob.

"Hello, Jack," said the small figure.

"She doesn't know you're called Dez," whispered Yakob, leaning forward.

"You are now safely in the hands of one of our best agents," Tor Kobal continued. "And it is time for me to tell you why…"

The next half-hour was the most extraordinary of Dez's life.

Priam IV's star system, Tor Kobal told him, was dominated by two cultures, the Tylurians and the Väd-Raatch. These two had been sworn enemies for longer than anyone cared to remember, and the Tylurians, according to Tor Kobal a peace-loving race, had managed to keep the Väd-Raatch at bay and their home planet safe until very recently. The arrival on the scene of a bloodthirsty new leader had changed the Väd's tactics. They were now at war.

This man's one aim in life was the destruction of the Tylurians and the devastation of Priam IV. To guard against this ever happening a secret weapon had been developed, but never actually made. The weapon – a complex, oxygen-hungry bacteria – could wipe out the Väd-Raatch in a matter of weeks once released on their planet. The plans, said Tor, were hidden in a safe place – in fact, split up into three parts and put somewhere the Väds would never find them. They were only to be used in the most extreme emergency, for the threat of the weapon's existence was enough to ensure peace.

So far, so good, except that the Tylurians had discovered there was a Väd spy in their midst. They didn't know who it was, or how much he, or she, had found out, until the person was intercepted trying to download information from the Tylurian High Command's central intelligence unit – a sort of computer like a cross between an ultra-bright plant and very clever rock.

The spy – obviously someone very high up in the Tylurian government able to gain access to the intelligence unit – was disturbed before he could get the information he was after. Realizing that he'd been rumbled he'd shut down his own terminal before the security forces could find out where he was operating from, and therefore who he, or she, was.

He had escaped detection, but not before breaking into the sector that contained part of the information about where the plans were hidden; then, when it seemed as if he was about to be caught, he'd infected the Tylurian computer with a deadly bio-metric virus – a disease that had damaged, beyond repair, almost all the other files about the secret plans. The data they contained had been lost for ever.

The tiny holographic figure of Tor Kobal paused for breath. Dez looked at Yakob.

"What's all this got to do with me?" he asked.

"Wait, there's more," Yakob said.

"You are probably wondering what all this has to do with you, Jack." Tor started talking again and Dez found himself nodding at the hologram, even though it couldn't see him. "And the reason is that we hid the inform-ation about our secret weapon – including the antidote – on your planet. To be exact, some eleven years ago we placed it in the genetic coding of three inhabitants of Earth. You are one of them." The figure pointed in his general direction and then froze. Dez noticed that Yakob was touching part of the console, almost as if he was tapping out a phone number on a keypad that wasn't there.

"Are you all right?" he asked. "Shall I start the holo again?" Dez nodded. He wasn't all right! He was, to put it mildly, stunned. Eleven years ago? He'd only had his eleventh birthday three months before. He'd been messed around with by aliens when he was only three months old? No wonder he couldn't remember it happening! But how come no one else knew? Did this have anything to do with him being an orphan? A million questions raised their hands and demanded to be asked, but you couldn't talk to a hologram, only listen. He watched Yakob touch the surface of the console again.

"Hidden in the double helix, the twin spirals of your DNA, is one-third of the information required to make the secret weapon we need to stop the Vad Raatch," Tor continued. "You may not believe this is possible, you may not believe that we could have done this – but you are sitting in a vehicle that has travelled well over a quarter of a million light years to find you, so please believe that *every* word I say is the truth.

"We thought we had chosen a hiding place the Väds would never find, but we hadn't reckoned on the traitor. We were lucky the spy was uncovered before he found out everything, although what he got was bad enough. He had managed to get your name and where you were – that was all. When we searched through the mess our central intelligence unit's memory was in, we found that all we now had was the same information the spy got, plus the names of the other two people and the cities in which they lived. They would be difficult to find, but not impossible.

"The race was then on to get to you before the Väds. They wanted you dead, and if you died we would not be able to build our weapon. You three are like pieces of a jigsaw puzzle – the picture is incomplete, and the information useless, without all of you being alive.

30

"I must end now. I am glad Yakob has succeeded, and I look forward to meeting you in person in the very near future."

The hologram saluted, and then faded to nothing. Dez stared at the empty black circle, finding it hard to blink, let alone think. Tylurians? Väd-Raatch death squads? People from a planet three hundred thousand light years away? He had to be hallucinating, but he knew he wasn't. This was real, this was happening. And what was more, it was happening to him, Dez Danby, 14 Avenscroft Road (until he moved), London, England, Northern Hemisphere, Earth, the Solar System.

He breathed out and realized that he'd been holding his breath for ages. He looked at Yakob. Yakob raised his eyebrows, as if to say "Well?" and Dez rubbed his face with his hands before speaking.

"So, I'm a filing cabinet."

"Excuse me?"

"Your lot thought I'd make a neat place to

store stuff…" Dez frowned. "How'd they come to choose *me*?"

"I've no idea, Dez. I was still in the Academy eleven years ago." Yakob pressed the silver holo-chip and there was another T-ssst! as it disengaged from the bobbled surface of the console. He picked it up and put it away. "All I know is, now I've found you, I have to tell Tor Kobal so she can send one of *Tyson's Grip*'s cruisers here to pick you up."

"Tyson's grip? What's that?"

"The T-class Star-Jumper we came here in – it's hidden out behind the planet you call Pluto at the moment." Yakob swivelled his chair and turned to face the console. "Excuse me for a minute, would you?"

Dez watched as Yakob's hands moved like dancing spiders across the surfaces in front of him. As he watched he could hardly believe what he saw – things moved, other things disappeared and the whole area in front of Yakob seemed to reform into a new configuration. Then Yakob started speaking; it still sounded like total gibberish, but then it was a foreign language. About as foreign as you could get, thought Dez, making a mental note to ask how the talking bit worked.

"Done!" said Yakob, sitting back.

"What is?"

"I've just sent a hyper-fast coded message to *Tyson's Grip* informing them that I have you in safe keeping."

"What happens now?"

"I will tell you…"

Chapter 4

Sitting holding a cup of something hot (coffee? tea? Tylurian mushroom soup? who knew?) that Yakob had given him, Dez listened to "the plan".

They were going to drive from the Dordogne to a pre-arranged site in the Alps, where a cruiser from *Tyson's Grip* would come and pick Dez up. Yakob would then go and find the other two people who had the code inside them.

"Why do we have to drive?" asked Dez, putting his empty cup down. Whatever he'd been drinking had actually tasted quite nice. "If you're such an advanced lot, why can't this van, or whatever it is, just teleport us there?" He snapped his fingers.

"It *can* fly," said Yakob, "but the cloaking device isn't working properly. As far as the diagnostics can tell one of its logic buffers has lost the plot. It *thinks* it's working, but it isn't."

"It was working all right when I walked into the thing!" interrupted Dez.

"That's because it only works properly when we aren't moving. I don't want to alert anyone to the fact that we're here by flying – your people or the Väds."

"Why would the Väds still be here? They think I'm dead."

Yakob fiddled with one of the controls and something, somewhere in the van, started to hum quietly. "Remember the spy?" he asked. Dez nodded. "He's still there in Central Command; he wasn't caught. If he finds out you are still alive we'll be in the firing line again."

"So," said Dez, getting up and walking over

to look at the driving compartment, "you can't talk to your ship, except in hyper-fast code; we can't fly, and the Väds might still be out there looking for me." He turned. "Have you got a gun, just in case?"

"I carry a needle laser; the van has side-mounted, melt-tipped rockets, front and rear Cold Pulse cannon and three-ply molecular shielding, just in case."

"And a broken cloaking device."

"Yes, and a broken cloaking device that will be fixed as soon as the cruiser arrives. Look," Yakob got up and walked past Dez and sat in the driving seat, "you're safer here than anywhere else on this planet."

"I'd be even safer if you hadn't mucked around with me and made me into a target for a bunch of space gangsters who ended up killing my parents!" Dez did what he'd been wanting to do since getting into the van. He kicked something. Whatever it was simply absorbed the shock by letting his foot sink into it slightly, making him feel a bit foolish.

"I can only apologize for what has happened to you," said Yakob, ignoring Dez's outburst. "I'm sure that when Tor finds out how badly things have gone wrong she'll be horrified. It was never meant to be like this – never."

"Well, it is like this, and this is supposed to be my holiday! Some rotten holiday." Dez plonked himself down in the seat next to Yakob. "I know it's not your fault, Yakob, but, you know, what's going to happen to me? I mean after this is all over?"

"I don't know. That is in the future. For now all I can say is that we must get to our destination within the next two days. When you meet Tor, you must ask her."

"Well, let's go," sighed Dez. "I've never seen an Alp, so I suppose that's something to look forward to."

"You are a brave kid, Dez," said Yakob, flicking switches on the dashboard as he spoke. The lights in the van went out and the headlights switched on, illuminating the trees in front of them. He reached over with his right hand, taking Dez's hand and shaking it. "I am very pleased to have met you, and only sorry that it is in such bad circumstances."

"Me, too," replied Dez, smiling despite how he felt. There was something about this man that made him unable to stay angry with him for long. Then a thought struck him. "Has this thing got number plates and everything, in case we get stopped by the cops?"

Yakob muttered something in his own language and started turning the very un-alien-looking steering wheel. "Yes it has," he grinned, looking at the windscreen, which now showed the view out of the back window as the van reversed, "but thanks for the reminder!"

Once Yakob had driven the van out of the clearing and on to a rough track, he spoke again. Instantly the windscreen cleared and Dez found himself looking at the real view in front of him.

"How…?"

Yakob shrugged. "Muta-cyte webs sandwiched between two layers of plex," he said. "The new model will have a Tri-D upgrade." None the wiser, Dez nodded anyway as Yakob spoke in his own language again and a map appeared, low down on the windscreen. A red dot blinked in the bottom left-hand corner and a green one to the right. He pointed at the green one. "That's where we have to go."

"How far is it?"

"550–600 kilometres – about a day's drive."

"But we don't have to be there for two days," said Dez. "What're we going to do for the rest of the time?"

"If we get there early, we rest. It's always good to have some spare time."

Dez nodded, thinking that Yakob sounded just like his father – far better to be early and have to wait for hours than be even five minutes late for anything. He watched as the van moved quickly along the deeply rutted forest track, its suspension making it feel as if they were driving over the smoothest of motorways.

"You will drive carefully," he said, as the memories of – how long ago? An hour, two hours? He couldn't be sure – came back.

"Very carefully," replied Yakob. "You are—"

"I know, '*safer here than anywhere else on this planet*' ... but just watch out for big trucks."

From the forest track they turned on to a small side road, and from that on to a two-lane road with the occasional farmhouse, shuttered against the night, just visible against the skyline. An hour later they were still travelling along the same type of road, not fast, not slow. Poodling.

"Why don't you get on to a motorway? You know – an autoroute. Wouldn't that be quicker?" asked Dez.

"Could be, probably, but I prefer to stick to the less well-travelled routes."

"Just in case?"

"Yes," smiled Yakob, "just in case."

Dez fell silent, looking out of his side window. The van was a left-hand drive, like a proper continental car, and for some reason this made him feel safer. Looking back inside the van he noticed there was no rear-view mirror; he was just about to comment on this when he saw it had a small rear-view screen instead. And in it Dez could see a police car – at least he *hoped* it was a police car. "Yakob," he said nervously, "we're being followed."

"I know, I've just done a scan. It's an ordinary car; I can't pick up anything unusual."

"Could it be the Väds?" asked Dez.

"It could, but they'd have to be unarmed."

"Why?"

"Because pleraniar vauschite gives off high resonance feedback when sonascanned," replied Yakob, his eyes flitting to and from the rear-view screen.

"Oh..." said Dez.

"PV, the plasmetal that laser weapons are made of, has a particular sound signature when scanned." Yakob accelerated the van, and the car behind also speeded up. "And that car has no shielding. I'd know if they were carrying."

"I see," nodded Dez, who did, sort of. "What will we do if they stop us?"

"Act dumb."

"One of my many talents," said Dez.

"Happily," said Yakob, pointing to one of the dashboard screens, "I don't think we're going to have to put it to the test – they've just received a radio message calling them away."

From just behind them a loud siren began to wail and Dez jumped as he saw the police car's blue light begin to flash. Seconds later the white saloon car sped past the van and away into the night. As the red tail lights disappeared Dez realized his hands were tightly balled and slowly he unclenched them.

"Try and relax," said Yakob. "We've a long way to go and you're going to be a nervous wreck if you do that every time there's a car behind us. Why don't you tell me about yourself?"

Dez looked at Yakob. "What do you want to know?"

"Oh, you know, everything – what it's like being you, here on Earth." Yakob checked the mini rear-view screen in front of him and overtook the battered 2CV bumbling along ahead of them. "Loud, noisy, dirty, inefficient – why do they make things like that, let alone buy them? Sorry, talking to myself. You were going to say?"

"I don't know what to tell you," frowned Dez. "I'm just a kid. I don't do anything except fool around and go to school … fool around *at* school as well." He sat back and let the seat hug him like a big, fat auntie at a christening. "Well, I'm eleven – but you know that. I like football, computer games, pop music and watching TV. I've got a dog called Rufus, two best friends – Tim and Cy – and I'm moving schools in September. Which is all right, 'cos I didn't really like the one I was at, but not all right 'cos I'm even less sure about the new one. And I'm moving house, which is definitely *not* all right, 'cos Tim and Cy won't be there." He paused. "Well, I *was* moving house and schools, but now … you, know, who knows?"

"But what's it like living here?"

"I don't live here," Dez explained. "I live in Britain. This is France, and I've no idea what it's like to live here. They eat lots of garlic and go '*Je t'aime les bicyclettes de Belsize,*' and stuff like that."

"OK, what's it like living in Britain?"

"S'all right; doesn't rain half as much as people say it does. We've got a crap football team and my dad says – my dad *said* – that we've got a bunch of crooks running the country," Dez turned in his seat. "Now you tell me what it's like on Priam IV – you can see what it's like here."

Yakob laughed, slapping the steering wheel as he did so. "Well said, Dez! Good point!" He sat back in his seat and, flicking a switch, took his hands off the steering wheel and turned to look at his passenger.

"What are you *doing*? The road – look at the road!"

"It's all right, this steering wheel's really just for show, so we don't look conspicuous. I've put the machine on auto," grinned Yakob. "It's a better driver than me anyway, and now I can concentrate on talking to you."

"Machines go wrong, like cloaking devices, remember?"

"Trust me," said Yakob.

"I was always told never to trust strangers."

"And what could be stranger than a man who says he comes from behind the Cygnus Rift?"

Dez nodded.

"OK, *I'll* drive," sighed Yakob, turning back to the wheel. "Where were we? Oh, yes, Priam IV. Well, it's bigger than your planet, has four moons and is in a system with twin suns – sunset takes for ever and we have slightly shorter nights than days.

"Many thousands of your years ago we shared the planet with the Väds – there was enough room for everyone. There were wars

45

(there are always wars) but we co-existed, lived together quite well, really. But after one particularly vicious war (one that the Väds lost badly) they packed their bags, so to speak, and left Priam. It took them some years to do, but they went and colonized another planet in our system – Anavrin – and made it their own.

"Strange to tell, they *still* had wars – terrible, cataclysmic battles amongst themselves that have turned parts of Anavrin into nuclear dustbowls. I suppose they must just like fighting."

"Don't you have any wars on Priam, then?" asked Dez. "We have them all the time here. I suppose we must like them as well. Are *we* like the Väds?"

"We don't have big wars," replied Yakob, looking over at Dez. "And, no, you people here are nothing like the Väds."

"But what's Priam like? Is it a nice place?"

"It's not perfect," said Yakob. "Nothing ever is; but some parts of it are beautiful, truly beautiful — even some of the cities, and it's hard to make a city attractive. Too many people all wanting to do different things.

"Priam is a very advanced place, in comparison to Earth, as you've probably guessed." Yakob indicated the van they were travelling in, and Dez nodded, even though to call the thing he was sitting in "advanced" seemed to him to be like calling a Ferrari "quite fast". Super-futuristic might come closer. "But we haven't forgotten where we came from. We still have countryside, we still have waterfalls and wild animals — they just look rather different from the ones you have here."

"The ones we still have left," mused Dez. "We don't seem to be very good at remembering where *we* came from."

"Do you want to hear more?" Yakob inquired.

"You bet! What about school? Do you have schools up there?"

"Do we have *schools*!"

And as the darkened countryside sped past, the van eating up the distance between them and the Alps, Dez sat and listened, spellbound, to this strange man from beyond the stars spin tales of life on an alien planet.

Chapter 5

When Dez woke up he found the sun shining through the van's tinted windows and his seat tipped back, almost like a bed. He felt completely rested and ravenously hungry.

He yawned. "When did I fall asleep?"

"Just before dawn. I'll never get used to just one sun – very odd!"

Outside Dez could see that they were still travelling on a smallish country road, fields on either side, some with crops, some with animals. It all looked very – what was that phrase he'd heard? – very chocolate box.

"Where are we?"

"Outside somewhere called Lyon."

"What time is it?"

Yakob looked at his wrist. "Nearly 11.30, Earth time."

"What? Almost lunch and I haven't even had breakfast yet! Can we stop for some food?"

"We don't have to," Yakob pointed behind him. "I've got food here."

"But have you got a croissant – or better still, a glass of milk, eggs and bacon and a slice of hot buttered toast? That's the question."

"The short answer to that is 'no', but I do have a cup of mezz, some plakk and frew or a slice of tasmang. How about that?"

"I could eat a horse, so I suppose a plate of plakk and frew won't hurt me." Dez sat up and his seat sat up with him. "It *won't* hurt me, will it?"

"There's only one way to find out," Yakob smiled. "Are you going to let me put *Stark Revenge* on auto so I can get you some food, or am I going to have to stop?"

"Stark revenge? What's that?"

"The best translation of this van's name that I can come up with – I've been thinking about it all night."

"What does it mean? It doesn't make sense," said Dez.

"Mean? It doesn't *mean* anything. What does Jack Danby mean? Names are simply labels, something you give to a person or an object that makes it different from another one. They don't have to make sense; they just avoid confusion."

"S'pose so… Look, I think you'd better stop. I mean, the sight of this thing driving itself is going to look, you know, *odd*. We might have got away with it in the dark, but—"

"You're right," said Yakob, pulling the van over to the side of the road and stopping. "So, plakk and frew and a cup of mezz?"

"If that's what's on the menu."

Yakob walked into the rear of the van. "When you're hungry, anything tastes good. I'm sure that's as true here as it is on Priam."

"We'll see," replied Dez, looking round at *Stark Revenge*'s cabin. "Does this thing have a radio?"

"Who do you want to talk to?"

"I don't want to talk to anybody; I want to listen to some music." Dez suddenly remembered his bum-bag. His hands grabbed his waist and he looked down; it was still there, scuffed but intact. He unzipped it and took out his Walkman. Amazingly enough, it seemed to have survived being thrown out of the car and bounced across a road. He unwound the tiny earphones, put them on and pressed "start". "Now, *that's* what I call music!" he said out loud, as the tape began to play.

"And this is what I call food," said Yakob, coming back into the cabin and handing Dez a plate with two yellow squares of something and a light blue circular slice of something else on it. They were hot.

Dez turned off the tape. "*Blue* food?"

Yakob sat down and started driving. "Close

your eyes and it's just food."

Not long after Dez had finished his "meal" –
even though it had tasted OK, he was still
having trouble thinking of it as proper food –
he noticed that there seemed to be rather
more traffic in front of them than before. The
road was quite twisty, and had hedges on
either side, so they couldn't see very far
ahead.

Yakob was using the Walkman, fascinated
by what he called its "crude technology", and
Dez wasn't at all sure he was paying too much
attention. He could even have put *Stark
Revenge* on auto without him knowing and be
pretending to drive while he listened to the
tape, a recent Top Ten compilation.

"Can you get the van to look round corners
and find out why we've slowed down?" he
asked, loudly, so Yakob could hear.

No reply.

"Yakob! Can you—"

"What?" The Tylurian stopped tapping the

steering wheel and took out the earphones. "Great music, but what does 'blow your mind' mean?"

"Be really amazed by, I think. I'm not sure. Lots of those songs have words just so you have something else to listen to." Dez pointed at the traffic. "Did you hear what I said? Can you make *Stark* see round corners and find out why the cars have slowed down?"

"I could fly over everyone, but that might cause a bit of a stir," said Yakob, peering through the windscreen. "We'll find out soon enough. Don't worry – we're doing fine for time."

As they rounded the next bend the road straightened out and they could see some kind of road block a few hundred metres in front.

"Now I can do something," Yakob said, turning on a piece of equipment set into the dashboard. A flat screen popped up and showed an image of what was happening in front of them. Yakob adjusted the controls and the picture became a close-up, with sound, of what was happening.

"*Excusez-moi, Monsieur; ça ne va pas vous prendre très longtemps, mais nous sommes à la recherche d'un évadé. C'est un criminel.*"

"Can you understand what he's saying?" Yakob pointed to a policeman who was wearing sunglasses and bending down to speak to the driver of the car at the head of the queue.

"I got 'could do a lot better if he tried' in my French report last term."

"No matter; we'll know soon enough – the queue's moving quite fast."

"Must be something quite big," mused Dez. "I can see four or five unmarked cars as well as the police one."

"The translator circuits have kicked in," said Yakob, as subtitles in a weird script began appearing at the bottom of the little screen. "It's something to do with an escaped criminal ... armed and dangerous. He's saying – the policeman – that no one should approach him if they see him, and don't pick up any hitchhikers. What's a hitchhiker?"

"Someone standing by the road, asking for a lift. Look, they're making the driver open the boot so they can check inside!"

"People travel in such small places here?"

"No, Yakob, they—"

"Only joking!"

"An alien with a sense of humour!" sighed Dez. "Don't joke with the policeman. My dad always said they thought you were up to something if you were too jolly – oh, no!"

"What's the matter?"

"What if they ask to see our passports and stuff? Mine's burnt to a crisp and you don't have one at all!"

"Not quite true. They gave me papers on the *Grip* before I left. I haven't even looked at them yet, to be honest." Yakob scratched his head. "Do you think they'd believe us if we said yours had been stolen?"

"Can't you kind of *make* one?" asked Dez, a worried look on his face. "I mean, if this mega-machine of yours can do breakfast, can't it magic up a passport?"

Yakob moved *Stark* forward a few metres as a car was let through the road block. It would be their turn in four cars' time. "If we had a little more time I'm sure it could, but not right now, I'm afraid."

"And you look nothing like my dad – they'll think I've been kidnapped or something!"

"You worry too much."

"I've got lots to worry about."

Three cars to go.

"Must be a bad man, this escaped criminal," said Yakob.

"Why?"

"Ten, maybe twelve men; lots of cars."

"Just like the movies."

"If you say so."

Two cars to go.

"Have you ever seen any space monsters?" Dez was getting bored with all the waiting.

"My Astro-Nav tutor at the Academy was one of the ugliest people I've ever met –

bad–tempered too."

"No, I mean – you know, like real monsters, with a hundred eyes and loads of tentacles, blasting ray guns and stuff. That kind of thing."

"Is that what you think it's like up there?" Yakob pointed and looked up at the roof of the van.

"That's what it's like in the comics."

"The comics sound more interesting."

One car to go.

Dez glanced at the rear view screen and then looked back more closely. There were no cars behind them, and only one in front. They were almost alone, in the middle of the French countryside and surrounded by heavily armed policemen. The car in front moved off.

Suddenly there was a hollow feeling in the pit of Dez's stomach. Something wasn't right, he didn't know what and he had no idea why. Maybe he *was* worrying too much, but maybe, just maybe, his survival instincts were turned full up. Was this a road block? Were these really policemen? The car in front disappeared from sight round a bend in the road.

"Scan them, Yakob," he said. "Do it now!" A split second later he saw the policeman with sunglasses turn and nod to the men behind him. "It's a trap!" he yelled. Everything was going in slow-motion once more, just like in the accident. He saw some of the policemen duck down into their cars, as if to pick something up, and as they stood he saw they were holding large, black things that could only be guns. They were like the kind you saw in sci-fi movies – only he was sure these weren't props. These guns looked as if they could burn a hole through a tank, possibly even three-ply molecular shielding.

Why wasn't Yakob doing anything? he thought, as the "policemen" slowly turned to point their guns at him – at *him!* his mind screamed.

"Väds..." he heard Yakob mutter. "You were right..."

"They're going to kill me!"

"Not if I have anything to do with it."

"But you're not *doing* anything!"

"Hold on," said Yakob. His arms straight out, his hands gripping the steering wheel, he yelled something at the top of his voice.

From being in a world where time had slowed down to a trickle, as if someone had hit his own personal pause button, Dez was suddenly thrown forcibly down into his seat. The cushion absorbed most of the shock, but he still felt as if his stomach had been nailed to the road while the rest of him reached for the sky.

Out of the window the road, the policemen, their guns, cars – everything had disappeared. All he could see was blue, and for a very long moment he had no idea what had happened. Then his brain caught up with reality. *Stark Revenge* had taken off. Vertically. It felt like 0–200 metres in next to no time.

"Don't *ever*…" he said through gritted teeth, as Yakob yelled something in the general direction of the dashboard and he was pushed hard, back into his seat, "...try this at home, kids..."

Chapter 6

Stark Revenge was flying. How far off the ground, Dez had no idea, but everything looked incredibly tiny and a long way down. He'd flown before, but never in anything this small. Never in a van, for heaven's sake! All around him those strange trilling voices babbled away, the windscreen was covered in flashing, blinking displays, and lights – red, green, yellow, blue – winked on the dashboard while screens showed ever-changing exterior views.

Dez noticed one screen in particular. The camera – if that was what it was – must have been quite close to him, and it gave a view along the side of *Stark*. He could hardly believe his eyes. The van was no longer van-shaped! As he watched, it was changing. What was that program he'd seen on Cy's brother's computer? The one that he'd used to make a picture of his father turn into a pig? Morphing, that was it! And he was watching *Stark Revenge* do it, right in front of him — not turn into a pig, but an aircraft.

"The van!" he exclaimed, turning to look at Yakob. "It's changed shape!"

"Well, *you* try flying something the shape of a box. It's possible but no fun, I can tell you!"

Dez looked out of the window again. The sides of the van had curved out to make short, stubby wings, and a rear-view monitor showed that they'd "grown" a small tailplane. As far as he could see, the skies were clear. They'd got away.

"Phew! That was close!"

"It still is," muttered Yakob, his eyes flicking all over the dash as he spoke, his hands whipping out to make a small adjustment here and turn something on (or off, Dez couldn't tell) there.

"What d'you mean?" Dez looked around frantically. Nothing to be seen. Not even a bird. "Where?"

Yakob indicated a pattern of pulsating lights on the dash. "We've got company," he said, turning up the zoom on the rear-view screen when the van bucked sideways. "Pulse beam ... there they are."

Dez saw a couple of evil-looking black helicopter-type craft on the screen. He couldn't tell if they were gaining on them or whether the camera was still zooming in. Whichever it was, the things were far too close. "How come we can see them? Can't they cloak their stuff?"

"They can, but they obviously don't care if they're seen. Look," he said, "you may want to close your eyes. I'm going to have to fling *Stark* around a bit."

"Are we going to die?"

"You want the truth?" The van shook again. "Or—"

"The truth."

"I don't know," said Yakob. The steering wheel was juddering and he was gripping it tightly with both hands. "But we'll soon find out."

Dez didn't close his eyes, but he didn't look out of the windows or at the screens either. He kept his eyes firmly on Yakob, aware that his seat was holding him so tightly that he couldn't have got out of it even if he'd wanted to. The thought passed through his head that he wanted to go to the loo. Badly. Then, before he had a chance to think anything else, the van, or what it had turned into, turned a somersault and then looped the loop.

At least that's what it felt like. Dez had once been on a massive roller-coaster ride at a theme park somewhere (right then he couldn't remember where, and couldn't care less). That ride had frightened the life out of him in an exhilarating kind of way, the kind of way that made him go back for a second turn almost as soon as he'd got off. He'd thought he was about to die, and it had occurred to him how silly it was to pay to be scared. He'd give anything to be anywhere else, anywhere in the whole world, rather than where he was at the moment.

It felt as if the van was being flung about like a squash ball in a grudge match, flying like an insect does — left, right, right some more, upside down and then coming to a stop in mid-air and spinning round. The taste of plakk and frew rose in his throat. The last thing he wanted to do was be sick. Correction, the *second*-to-last thing he wanted to do was be sick. Mostly, he didn't want to die.

"Why don't you shoot at them with those melt-tipped thingies of yours?"

"I'm too busy trying not to be shot *at*, is why." Yakob whistled softly as a group of lights on Dez's side of the dash flared up. "That was close!"

"What was?" Dez whirled round, and

somewhere in front of them a shimmering, glassy sphere of air exploded silently.

"PhotoSonic cluster. Would've made quite a dent in the shielding."

"How come they keep missing?"

"I was top of my Evasive Action class," smiled Yakob grimly.

"No one could catch you?"

"Ninety-nine out of a hundred times."

Stark dipped and skewed, almost skidding in the air as another glassy ball shattered to Dez's right, much closer than the last time.

"They're good," Yakob grunted, powering *Stark* forward again. "But I've got a feeling I'm better."

"I hope it's more than a feeling," Dez muttered to himself, grabbing the sides of his seat. There was a sudden jolt, all the lights dimmed and the sky went a deep, deep blue and then back to normal.

"Fooled them!" yelled Yakob, as *Stark* appeared to start flying backwards.

"Are we, you know, going back the way we came now?"

"In a manner of speaking." Yakob was hunched forward over the steering wheel, staring intently at the map on the windscreen. "We just warped slightly."

"Warped? As in 'Warp factor 5, Mr Sulu'? Like on *Star Trek*?"

"I wouldn't know about that. More like being on page one hundred of a book and turning back to page ninety-eight." Yakob slapped the dashboard. "Yes! Got it!"

"*Time* travel? We went back in *time*?"

"Only a second or two, just enough to confuse the heck out of the Väds."

"Me too," said Dez. "Where— *Woo-o-o-ow!* Where are we going now?" The van was falling, nose first, in what seemed to him like a kamikaze dive straight for a large expanse of forest.

"Somewhere safe, safer than being up here anyway," replied Yakob, as the trees rushed towards them. Just before it seemed inevitable that they would crash, Yakob pulled *Stark* up and they dropped slowly through the tangle of leafy branches, finding a space to go through where, from way up in the air, it had seemed impossible.

The next thing Dez knew, the van was sitting, rocking gently on whatever it used for suspension, in a tiny clearing deep in the forest. Yakob lowered *Stark*'s side windows, letting in the sounds and smells of the quiet, peaceful woodland, and then punched in the command for it to morph back into its van shape. Dez leaned out of his window and watched as the metallic wings disappeared soundlessly, flowing back into the main body of the vehicle in the same way as mercury moves on a dish in the science lab.

"How does it do that?"

"Intelligent metal. It can memorize shapes," explained Yakob. "It has a built-in library of a dozen or so configurations – things it can become. Quite useful, really."

"I think my dad would have called that an

understatement."

"I think your dad would have been right. Get back in, Dez – I'm going to cloak."

Dez sat back down and Yakob said something. They both sat in silence for a few seconds, their minds a blank, listening to the sounds that make up a natural silence – the type of things you never hear because even thinking shuts them out…

THUD!

"What was that?" Dez whirled round. "Have they found us?"

"No; it was only a bird flying into the side of the van."

"How d'you know?"

"Saw it coming on the screen."

"You could have warned me!" Dez looked out of the window. He'd never seen what *Stark* looked like when it was cloaked – not in broad daylight, anyway. It was pitch black when he'd walked into it. "Can I get out and have a look at us being invisible?"

"No point. Nothing to see," grinned Yakob.

"They're still out there somewhere. And they're still looking for us. I don't want to give their sensors anything that might let them know where we are."

"How long are we going to have to wait?"

"As long as it takes." Yakob yawned and stretched. "Until it's dark, probably."

"I need to go to the toilet."

"Back there." Yakob pointed with his thumb. "Square thing with a lid."

Dez got up. "Don't look."

"I promise."

"There aren't any cameras pointing at me, are there?" He lifted the lid, undid his trousers and sat down.

"None."

"You don't recycle this stuff, do you?" he asked as some paper spooled out of a slot in the wall next to him.

"Don't be disgusting!"

"Just checking!" he laughed. There was a soft hiss and a small hatchway opened up in front of him. "What's that for?"

"Put your hands inside for a moment," said Yakob. "It'll clean them."

Dez did as he was told. "All mod cons," he said, returning to his seat.

"'*Like taking your house with you*', we say – very roughly translated."

"'*A home from home*', we say," smiled Dez.

"Perfect! A home from home – exactly!" Yakob got up. "Now it's your turn not to look."

Dez sat back and looked at the life going on outside the cloaked van. Whatever panic their arrival had created amongst the animals in this part of the forest, they seemed to have forgotten about it now. He'd seen squirrels, a fox and a host of birds all going about their own particular business by the time Yakob came back, holding two cups of steaming liquid.

"Definitely not recycled," he said, handing one to Dez.

"What did you say this was called?" he asked as he took a sip.

"Mezz."

As Yakob was sitting down the dashboard lit up like a Christmas tree, and Dez got the distinct impression that *Stark* was actually tensing itself, getting ready for something to happen.

"Overflight," said Yakob, bending over to look up out of the van's sloping windscreen.

"The Väds? But ... but I thought we'd lost them?"

"We did, but they know we're still here somewhere." Yakob examined various readouts on the dash. "And these boys don't give up that easily."

"What's *Stark* doing?" asked Dez, who could hear things happening all around him.

"It's dissipating heat from everything, including us – bringing the temperature down so it's the same as our surroundings. That way it doesn't look like we're here."

"I thought we were cloaked and no one could see us."

"We are, and no one can see us, but we still

73

have what's called a heat autograph, and that can be picked up quite easily."

Dez shivered slightly. He didn't know if it was simply panic or the van cooling down. "Where are they?"

"Very low and right above us."

In Dez's mind's eye he could see the crouched black shapes of the Väd craft hovering in the sky like evil mosquitoes, waiting to strike. If they found them they would do more than bite – he knew that. One blast of PhotoSonic pulses and *Stark* would be history. He felt as if he was waiting outside the office of the Headmaster from Hell, but no amount of extra padding would save him now if the Väds discovered where they were.

He tried to swallow and found he couldn't. He glanced at Yakob. The man looked as if he was made out of stone. Dez felt as if *he* was constructed entirely out of jelly – pale, very frightened jelly.

Some lights on the dash flickered and

Yakob let out a small, low sigh. "They've gone," he said.

"Are you sure?"

"Without going up there and taking a peek, which I'm not going to do, I'm prepared to believe the tried and tested instrumentation installed in *Stark* which, I am told, has a fail factor of 0.00045 per cent. Yes, I am sure."

"What about the cloaking device?" muttered Dez.

"Give me a break, will you?" exclaimed Yakob. "Nothing's perfect!"

Whispers again. Shouted whispers. Angry whispers.

"*Report!*" they said.

"We lost them."

"*Explain.*"

"We think they warped."

"*Think?*"

"They warped, and by the time we realized what had happened, they'd hidden."

"Find them."

"We've tried."

"Try harder. Try much harder. Failure is not an option."

Chapter 7

"What now?" said Dez. "Are we safe?"

"Safe is a relative term."

"Don't understand."

"Well, we're safe enough where we are," said Yakob, "but we could be a lot safer elsewhere."

"Let's go then!" Dez clapped his hands together. "What are we waiting for? Step on the gas and accelerate *Stark* out of here!"

"Nothing's ever that easy, Dez."

"How did I know you were going to say that? All grown ups say things like 'nothing's ever that easy' and 'whoever said it was supposed to be fair' … even ones from Priam

IV," he sighed. "I thought at least you might be different."

"It's not me. I can't change the circumstances; I can only work with them."

"And what's that supposed to mean?"

"It means that we'll have to do some walking."

"*Walking?*" Dez wasn't too big on exercise of any description. "But it's *miles*! Why can't we drive there? If the Väds have gone we'll be all right, won't we?"

"I told you." Yakob stopped to take a sip from his cup. "Yeugh! I can't stand cold mezz!" He made a face, then lowered his window and threw the rest of his drink away. "Like I told you, the Väds don't give up easily. They'll be on the lookout for us everywhere. Even if *Stark* changed its shape they might pick us up. I daren't drive out of here."

"Won't walking be just as dangerous?" said Dez.

"No; the last thing they'll be expecting us

to do is leave our transport behind."

"You're going to abandon it?"

"No; I'm going to leave it here and come back and get it once I've delivered you."

"You make me sound like a parcel."

"No offence intended, but that's my job – delivering you to the scout ship from *Tyson's Grip* that'll be meeting us in around twenty-four hours from now."

"Twenty-four hours and at the top of an Alp from now!" Dez looked as if he'd chewed on a lemon. "How're we going to get there? You can't be serious about walking."

"Part of the way, yes. To the next big town. It's not that far, only twenty or so kilo-metres."

Twenty kilometres. Dez paused. For all that he'd been a metricated kid all his school life (and wouldn't know an ounce from a pint), when it came to kilometres he was lost. He'd never understood why his dad used to fill the car up with litres of petrol and then try to work out how many miles per gallon he was getting. Twenty – two times ten, five times four, count them – kilometres.

"How far's that?"

"It's twenty kilometres."

"I know that, but how long will it take us?"

"Oh, I don't know." Yakob looked at the map displayed on the windscreen. "Let's see … about, say, five or six hours if you're really slow."

"Five or six *hours*!" moaned Dez.

"Not all in one go, we'll stop about half-way and have a rest and some food."

"Oh, great! A midnight feast round the jolly old camp fire! I never joined the Boy Scouts because I hate all that camping lark. Are you positive we can't drive?"

"Positive," replied Yakob firmly. "It won't be so bad, although we can't have a fire as it might attract attention."

"Might keep us warm as well."

"I've got travelling packs; we'll be OK."

"The only travelling pack I'm interested in has four wheels and an engine."

"Are all boys like you?" Yakob looked him up and down.

"Like me how?"

"Lazy."

"I'm not lazy!"

"You just don't like walking, right?" grinned Yakob.

"Not for six hours in the dark." Dez sat round, facing the windscreen. Looking out of the front of the van he thought he saw something move. "Did you see that?"

"*Stark*'s been tracking it for the last few minutes."

"You never tell me anything!"

"You were too busy talking." Yakob got up and started to go into the back. "It's probably an animal or something."

"Wearing a *hat*?"

Yakob came stumbling back to his seat and looked in the direction Dez was pointing. Through the undergrowth, about a hundred metres away, they could see a man with a double-barrelled shotgun. Yakob muttered something and a screen popped up on the dash, its frame zooming in on the man as he raised one hand, took his hat off and scratched his head.

"Is that a Väd in disguise?" whispered Dez.

"I think not … that firearm looks like something from the Alter-Age." Yakob looked puzzled. "What's he doing out here with a thing like that?"

"Hunting, I suppose." Dez watched the man move carefully through the undergrowth, making almost no sound at all. "He's very good, isn't he?"

"At what?"

"Being quiet." The man turned and moved in their direction. "Has he seen us?"

"Not a chance."

"Why's he pointing his gun at us then?"

Yakob looked over his shoulder. "Look," he tapped Dez's arm and pointed out of the side window, "That's what he's seen."

"A deer!"

"If you say so, but if he fires and hits us –

which I assume he'll be able to do – he'll realize something's here."

"What can we do?"

"Watch." Yakob picked up his cup and threw it out of his window. Dez watched as it arced gracefully through the air and fell some way in front of the van. The noise spooked the deer, which scooted off, and made the hunter look away.

"*Merde!*"

A subtitle appeared on the small screen and Yakob smiled. "He wasn't pleased."

"No, but I bet the deer would be if it knew you'd saved its life," said Dez, watching the man skirt round the small clearing they were in and disappear into the trees in the direction the deer had taken.

"You drive vehicles whose motive power comes from a series of violent explosions, and you hunt with weapons that are about as accurate as throwing mud." Yakob raised his eyebrows and shook his head. "What a strange world you live in, Dez."

"What's wrong with the internal combustion engine?" They'd done a project on cars at the end of the summer term, so he knew what Yakob was talking about. "It works, doesn't it?"

"Just because something works doesn't mean it's good."

Dez was in no mood to start an argument about how good or bad car engines were. He was in no mood to start getting ready for a twenty-kilometre walk either, but, from the short time he'd known Yakob, he could tell when the man was being serious and when he was joking. They were going for a walk.

He looked at Yakob's clothes. Dark grey overalls and what appeared to be black running shoes with very thin soles – they might be all right for piloting a spiffy interstellar runabout, but…

"You're going to stick out like a sore thumb." Dez waved a finger at Yakob's clothes.

"I'm sorry?"

"Your clothes. They don't look right."

"What's wrong with them?"

"Here on Earth they're not the kind of thing you go for country walks in, that's all."

"And what you're wearing is?" Yakob looked Dez up and down, taking in his T-shirt, jeans, trainers, bum-bag and the sweatshirt he had tied round his waist.

"Yeah."

"Stand up for a moment, would you?" Dez stood up. "Turn round slowly." Dez turned round, and as he did so Yakob said something in his own language.

"Fashion show over?" asked Dez. "Can I sit down?"

"Sure." Yakob got up and went into the back of the van. "I'll be back in a minute. Watch the instruments."

"What for?"

"Väds."

"But I—" squeaked Dez.

"Just my little joke!" Yakob said from the back of *Stark*, where Dez could hear the sound of something whirring and clicking.

He wanted to look, but couldn't take his eyes off the dashboard.

"What do you think?" asked Yakob, re-appearing. He was wearing a T-shirt, jeans, trainers, bum-bag and sweatshirt tied round his waist, just like Dez – in fact *identical* to what Dez was wearing, right down to the last scuff and crease.

Dez was silent for a second, and then he burst out laughing, giggling at first and then really letting rip. All the tension that had built up since his parents' death and the attack at the road block dissolved as he fell about, clutching his sides.

"Is something wrong?"

"No, nothing! It's just that…"

"What?" Yakob looked down at himself and then up at Dez. "Didn't *Stark* do a good job?"

"It did too good a job – we'll look a right pair!"

"A right pair of what? Please explain; I don't see the joke."

"Well," said Dez, calming down, "I don't

suppose it's *that* funny, but we'll look like identical twins, sort of."

"This is a bad thing?"

"This isn't a good thing when one of us is so much shorter than the other. Hang about." Dez got up and took off his sweatshirt, turned it inside out and put it on. Then he opened his bum-bag, took out a crumpled baseball hat and put it on back-to-front. "There, that should do it."

"No one will laugh at us now?"

"Not unless one of us steps on a banana skin."

Chapter 8

Dusk had just started to fall when Yakob said that it was time to go. They left *Stark Revenge*, cloaked and in maximum security mode, in the tiny clearing. Before leaving Yakob had squirted a coded message to *Tyson's Grip*, saying the meet was still on, and reminding Tor Kobal that he needed a new cloaking device.

Each was carrying a small dark green haversack, packed with food and other Tylurian survival essentials, some of which Yakob found he didn't have the words to explain. Dez felt a bit cold as they set off, but once they'd got into their stride he realized he was quite warm, and even thought he might have to take his sweatshirt off.

They kept mostly to small forest tracks, crossing main roads only when they had to, and then only when there were no cars coming. Occasionally Yakob consulted a small electronic map, whose coloured screen glowed in the dark. As they walked, they talked – it seemed to Dez almost non-stop. They talked about everything and anything: life on Earth, life on Priam IV, food, drink, school, girls, schoolgirls – you name it, they discussed it.

Only after they'd been walking for an hour or so, and a sickle moon had risen in the night sky, did Dez realize that Yakob had got him round to talking about the accident and his parents – two subjects that had been hovering in the back of his mind but he hadn't been allowing himself to think about.

"What were they like, your parents?" It was a simple enough question, but it made Dez stop walking when Yakob asked it.

"I've never really thought about them like that," he replied. "They were just, you know, *there*. It's hard to imagine that they aren't now. Too many things have been happening for it to sink in properly."

"It will take some time."

"But not being there is for ever, Yakob." Dez started to walk again. "I mean, you can't get *Stark* to warp again – to when they were alive – and stop the accident, can you?"

"No, I can't. I wish I could, but anything more than the couple of seconds' jump we did back there would be a serious time-effect warp. Even if it were possible, it could be dangerous and wouldn't solve anything, anyway."

"Why not?"

"Someone once worked it out – some really clever scientist called Chey Porr. She developed a theory – the Whole Story Theory, she called it."

"What did it say?" Dez jumped over a fallen tree.

"It said that everything that was going to happen *would* happen, no matter what you did."

"Why bother then?" asked Dez, looking back as Yakob stepped over the tree.

"A good question."

"I mean, if that was true, and I was going to pass all my exams, then why should I do any work at all?"

"Ah!" Yakob smiled. "But you *don't* know. None of us knows anything until it happens, and then it's too late. That's why you *have* to bother – that's why no one's ever managed to disprove the Whole Story Theory."

"Sounds like a cop-out to me. And anyway, if you can warp a little, what's so dangerous about warping a lot?"

"Warping one or two IOT's—"

"Eye–owetees?"

"Increments of Time – seconds to you ... anyway, warping one or two of those doesn't allow anything but the most infinitesimal changes to the Time Line. And changing the

Time Line isn't like simply changing your clothes – it affects everything for everybody and it's permanent. Apart from that it would take the most stupendous amounts of energy to do it, which even we don't have."

"Oh…"

"Do you understand?"

"I don't understand anything at the moment." Dez put both hands in his jeans pockets and hunched his shoulders. "I don't understand why I was chosen to have my DN blooming A messed around with, I don't understand why you Tylurians and the Väds can't do your fighting elsewhere, and I don't understand why I'm trudging through this *!*!* forest at the dead of night!"

"I think it's probably time to take a rest."

"Probably," humphed Dez. "Are we nearly there?"

"About half-way. We'll have some food, you sleep for a bit and then we'll get to the town around 9 o'clock tomorrow morning."

Yakob moved off the path and into the

brush, clearing a space where they could sit down. He shrugged off his haversack and took Dez's from him. The food he prepared wasn't like anything Dez had had before, but he was too tired to ask its name. He ate what he was given and just as he was about to lie down Yakob threw him a roll of something very light.

"Unwrap that and get inside," he said. "It'll keep you warm."

"What is it?"

"It keeps all your body heat in."

"Like a sleeping bag?"

"That would be a very good name for it." Yakob sounded as if he was smiling. "Sleep well."

Sleep is a strange thing. One moment you're wide awake, aware of everything around you, all the small noises sounding so much louder, and the next minute you're awake again. You don't know, if you can't see a clock, how long you've been sleeping. It could be minutes, it could be hours, and dreams that seem to last a lifetime can happen in the blinking of an eye.

When Dez woke up he had no idea what time it was or how long he'd been asleep. But he had a good idea what had woken him. As he fumbled to check his back-lit digital watch (4.30!) he could hear snuffling sounds coming from all round him.

"You awake?" whispered Yakob. It sounded as if his jaws were wired shut.

"Think so. What's happening?"

"I rather hoped you'd be able to tell me."

Along with the snuffling Dez could now hear trampling in the vegetation and the odd chewing and grunting noises. "I don't know." He peered into the darkness. "Probably animals." Wolves? he wondered. Did they still have them here?

"What kind of animals?"

"Hungry ones, I should say." From what Dez could remember, wolves seemed un-likely, and anyway they growled, didn't they?

Not grunted.

"I'll get my laser." Yakob sounded rattled.

"No, wait… It sounds like pigs."

"Is that good or bad?"

"Depends on the pig, I think." Dez sat up. "Have you got a torch?"

"What's a torch?"

"A light. Something so I can see what's going on."

"Oh!" Dez could hear Yakob fumbling in a haversack. "Are you sure this is wise?"

"Dunno about wise, but if you want to find out what's out there…" He felt Yakob give him something. "How do I turn it on?"

"Squeeze it."

Dez squeezed what felt like a cold rubber sausage and lit himself up. "Oops!" he grinned, turning the thing round and squeezing again. "Wow!"

A wide beam of light sprang out and lit up the brush. For a moment it was like looking at a flash photograph. Nothing moved. Then the scene came back to life as a dozen or so wild pigs wondered what to do next.

"What are they?"

"Pigs – wild pigs!" Dez could see the tusks on a big male glinting in the light.

"How wild is wild?"

"Wild as in 'not tame', not wild as in 'angry' … at least, not yet."

"How can you tell?"

"They're not coming towards us." Dez moved the beam left and right. "They're just out foraging, I think. We should be OK, we don't look like pig food."

"What does pig food look like?"

"Down on the farm, any old rubbish." Was he imagining things, or did Yakob sound scared? "Out here, I'm not too sure…" he went on, suddenly turning round to face Yakob, putting the torch under his chin and making a scary face. "*Wh-a-a-a-a-ah!!*"

"Aaagh!"

Yakob screamed and jumped up. Out in the brush Dez could hear the wild pigs scattering as if their lives depended on being somewhere else very fast indeed. He collapsed in a heap of laughter.

"That was unkind."

"It was a joke!" Dez spluttered, sitting up.

"Not from where I was sitting."

Dez shone the torch over towards Yakob, who was standing with his back to him. "I'm sorry," he said, getting up to join him. "I apologize."

"Accepted," said Yakob, turning to look at him. "You must remember that I am alone here too, a long way from home, and with the fate of my whole planet resting on my shoulders. You never asked to be a part of this and neither did I."

"They *made* you come here? You didn't volunteer?"

"It was my duty." Yakob put a hand on Dez's shoulder. "They told me I was the person best qualified. I had no choice."

"I thought only kids never got any choice – you know, got told what they were going to do." Dez looked up at Yakob and saw that he was staring up into the star-spattered sky. Out in the country, away from civilization, there were so many flickering pin-points of light it made him feel dizzy to look at it. "Where's Priam IV?"

"I've no idea," sighed Yakob. "It all looks so different from down here."

"How did you learn to speak English so well?"

"Are you trying to take my mind off things, or do you always make such sudden changes of subject?"

"All my teachers say I've got a butterfly mind, always flitting around." Dez handed the torch back. "Well?"

"I learnt it on the way here. I'm still learning it."

"Adults always say that."

"Say what?"

"You never stop learning." Dez shivered, picked up the thin sleeping bag and wrapped it round him.

"Adults are right, then."

"What a horrible thought! I'm fed up with learning *now* – I don't want to be doing it in twenty years' time!"

They waited and watched as the dawn came up, the skyline turning a delicate pale blue, seeping colour into the blackness. Around them things began to take shape, and what had been mysteries turned into boringly ordinary bushes and trees. There was no sign of the wild pigs. Whatever they'd been after near their camp site obviously hadn't been worth coming back for. Not with a screaming monster in residence.

With the rising sun warming them up by the minute, they sat and ate some food. Yakob did something to two foil packets and whatever was in them came out piping hot. The plastic bottles they carried held a clear fluid that tasted quite fruity, but Dez had no idea what sort of fruit.

"What wouldn't I give for a Coke right now!" he said as he finished off his drink.

"When we get to the town you can get one. What is it?"

"Fizzy-pop."

"Oh…" Yakob looked confused. "Good."

"Do you have adverts on Priam?" Dez asked as he got up and started to roll up his sleeping bag and repack his haversack.

"Adverts? You mean things that try to persuade you to buy products you don't necessarily want?"

"Or tell you about new stuff you haven't heard of."

"Yes, we have adverts," replied Yakob, putting on his haversack and checking that they hadn't left anything behind.

"You've got schools, you've got adverts — sounds a lot like being here."

"In many ways it is," agreed Yakob.

"Would I like it there?"

"If we make our rendezvous with the scout ship you'll have every chance to find out."

"I'm *going* there?" Dez stopped what he was doing. "You're taking me to Priam IV?"

"Not me personally … but yes, you will be taken there, with the others, to have the information you carry removed."

"Will it hurt?"

"Going there?"

"No!" Dez started to follow Yakob along the narrow track. "Having the information removed."

"No, it's a painless procedure."

"That's what they say about going to the dentist, but it's not true."

"This will be like going to sleep and waking up, that's all."

"And what will they do with the information once they've got it?" The track widened and allowed Dez to walk alongside Yakob instead of behind him.

"I suppose they'll make the weapon and maybe even use it."

"Who invented it?"

"Do you ever run out of questions?

"Haven't so far." Dez hitched up his backpack. "So, what's it going to be like when they set this secret weapon off? Are the Väds going to roll around gagging? Turn purple? Even better, turn inside out?"

"I don't know *how* it's supposed to work – it's a secret, no one's told me. Only the High Command know the details."

"And the spy and the Väds."

"True."

"Some secret!"

"True also."

They walked in silence for a time, and then came to a point where the track met a road. It was long and straight and shaded on one side by trees. Close to where they were standing Dez could see what looked like a bus stop, and in the distance, to his left, a single-decker bus was trundling towards them.

"Yakob?" he said, as the Tylurian was about to cross the road.

"Yes?"

Dez pointed to his right. "Is that the way to town?"

Yakob looked. "Uh–huh. Why?"

"Can we catch the bus, pl-e-e-e-ease?"

"We haven't got any money."

"*You* might not, but," Dez patted his bum-bag, "*I* have."

"You have?"

"Yes. Well, enough for the bus fare."

"All right," smiled Yakob. "I've never been on a bus."

Chapter 9

The bus was quite crowded, but they managed to get a seat each, one behind the other. It was going to a town called Chambéry, a few kilometres further than the town they'd planned to walk to, and luckily nearer their final destination — and Dez had just enough money for the tickets.

Up ahead they could see the road start its climb towards the snow-covered peaks. It looked cold up there, even though the sun was shining and it was getting hotter by the minute in the bus. The road they were on was following the course of a river, and the river was in full flow, fed by the melting snow from high up in the mountains.

Surrounded by the chatter and buzz of a motley collection of French people – grandmas, children, farmers and others – the two of them passed the time observing their fellow passengers and taking in the scenery. At some point the person next to Yakob got off and he moved over to the window and let Dez come and sit next to him.

Just after they'd driven past the sign telling them they were entering Chambéry, Dez noticed a car pulled off to the side of the road with its bonnet up. A man was sitting on the grille, not looking at the engine.

"Nice place to break down," Dez said. There was no reply from Yakob and Dez looked up at him. His face was serious. "What's the matter?"

"I want you to go and sit at the back of the bus by yourself."

"Why? We're nearly there. What would I want to do that for?"

"Because I think that man back there was a Väd – *don't* turn round!" Yakob began to talk very fast, bending down and whispering in Dez's ear. "Stay on the bus when I get off in the town centre – they'll be looking for two people, one of them a child. Get off at the next stop and find somewhere to stay out of sight. I'll come and get you."

"How? How will you find me?" Dez suddenly felt the happiness of the last few hours wash away, to be replaced by a creeping fear.

Yakob pressed what looked like a coin into his hand. "Don't lose this. I'll find you. Now go to the back and keep your head down!"

Again, like the first time they'd met, Dez felt an odd calmness, as if everything would be OK if he did exactly what Yakob said. As he walked to the back of the bus he glanced over his shoulder. Yakob was looking left and right out of the bus, watching the road like a hawk. As far as Dez could see, there were no other "broken-down" cars parked on the sides of the road.

He sat, hunched, on the back bench seat

opposite an old man whose garlic-flavoured smoke filled the air between them as he puffed on a fat yellow cigarette. He looked as if he wanted to talk, and Dez tried to ignore him. Dez looked at his watch. 11.30. They'd been on the go since just after dawn and ordinarily he'd have been starving. Now, though his stomach felt empty, it was a different kind of emptiness, one filled with butterflies and not requiring any sort of food at all.

The bus stopped.

Dez sat up slightly and watched a clutch of passengers get off, Yakob among them. He didn't look back or wave or anything. It was as if they'd never met and Dez had never felt so lonely in all his life. On top of everything else that had happened, now his only friend in the whole world (the entire *universe*) was walking off the bus.

The doors closed and the driver moved off.

"*Parlez-vous français?*"

Dez turned to the old man. "Me? No, I

mean *non*." He chewed his lower lip as he thought. "*Je*, um ... *je ne parle pas français, monsieur* ... sorry."

"I speak little Henglish," said the old man. "You very young to travel halone?"

"I'm meeting someone. They're, um, picking me up at the next stop." Dez's eyes darted sideways to look out of the bus window. There was no sign of Yakob. "I'm all right, really."

"*En vacance* ... on 'oliday?"

"Er, yes, holiday ... with my, um, parents." To Dez's horror, as the bus accelerated out of the town he saw another car by the side of the road, this time with its boot open, and a man standing by it with some tools in his hands. He sank down in his seat so that only his baseball cap would be visible.

"Are you feeling all right?" the old man rolled his R's as if he had a handful of gravel in his throat.

"Fine – a bit tired."

"You get out at ze next stop, you say?"

"The next stop, yes."

"Zere is *un café*. You would like maybe a sandwich?" The way the old man spoke it sounded more like *zaandweeech*, but Dez knew what he meant.

"Thank you, but—"

"No problem!" the old man smiled, showing an almost complete set of rather brown teeth. "It will be – 'ow you say? – my pleasure!"

What was it about him at the moment? thought Dez. Everyone he met wanted to be kind to him. Either that or they wanted to kill him. There was a loud hiss of air brakes, the engine beneath his feet roaring loudly as the bus slowed to go round a bend. Up ahead Dez could see a stop sign, right next to a small café, and beside him he was aware of the old man picking up a bag from the floor and getting ready to stand.

He had no choice – he had to get off with him. If he didn't Yakob might never find him, even with the tiny gizmo he had in his pocket.

He stood and let his latest friend go up the gangway to the door, following in his shuffling footsteps and waving a thick plume of smoke out of his face as he went.

Outside on the road he watched the twin doors *P–FFSST!!* shut and the bus drive off. He looked back the way they'd come. Who would be the first to arrive? Yakob, to pick him up, or a Väd death squad to make toast out of him? There were some things, he felt sure, that an 11-year-old boy (on holiday) shouldn't have to think about. And this was definitely one of them.

"*Mon p'tit, allons-y.* Come on, let us go." The old man pointed to the café. "I would like a glass of wine, and you, I'm sure, a sandwich."

Why did French people have such funny accents? he thought, as he went up the steps and into the café.

He was sitting with the old man, whose name was Armand, at a table near the window. He had demolished the most delicious ham sandwich he'd ever tasted and was on his second bottle of Orangina; Armand was on his third glass of wine and, Dez could hardly believe it, his *fifth* cigarette. The man's lungs must be waving little white flags. He hadn't eaten anything.

"Aren't you hungry?" asked Dez.

"*Non, non, non!*" wheezed Armand. "I heat zis hevening. I like my lunch in…" he pointed at his glass, waving his finger around.

"A glass."

"*Bien sur!* A glass!" Armand's laugh turned into a cough and he spat into a handkerchief that looked as if it had been around some time.

Dez was sure you could've been expelled for spitting at his school, and while Armand was being incredibly nice to him, he did wonder about some of his habits. He looked out of the window, checking the road for what seemed like the fiftieth time since he'd arrived. Not one other car had stopped or even slowed down, in the half an hour he'd been there.

"Your fazzer, 'e come?" enquired Armand.

"It's not my father, it's my, um, uncle." Dez had never been very good at lying; his ears always went red. They felt as if they were on fire now, although Armand didn't seem to notice.

"What car 'e 'as?"

"Not sure." He peered out of the window again and saw a dark blue saloon coming from the direction of the town, and as he watched one of its indicators started flashing as it slowed down. "Maybe this is him."

Armand leaned over the table to take a look. "Nice car zis new Citroën." He pronounced it *Si-trow-en*, nodding as he did so. "Ver' comfort-able."

Dez looked at the man getting out of the car. He was wearing a white floppy sun hat, dark glasses, khaki trousers and what looked like fairly serious walking shoes. Dez's heart sank. It wasn't Yakob. Then it sank even further as the ghastly thought occurred to him that it could well be a Väd.

He looked round the small café, his mouth suddenly dry. Was there a back entrance? Could he get to it in time? Would there be someone waiting for him if he did? Questions, questions…

"Is somesing ze matter?" asked Armand.

Dez was rooted to his chair, unable to move. He heard the hinges squeak as the café door opened. He didn't dare look round.

"Dez?" said a voice behind him.

It *was* Yakob! He could have leapt for joy as he turned to look. "Uncle!" Dez jumped up and ran over to him, hoping he wouldn't look too startled at being called such an odd name. "Thought you'd never get here!"

"Got caught in some traffic. Sorry I'm a bit late … aren't you going to introduce me?" Yakob took off his sunglasses and looked over at Armand, who was sitting at the table lighting yet another cigarette.

"Sorry," Dez turned round. "This is

Monsieur Armand; we met on the bus and he's been looking after me. I've had lunch."

To his absolute amazement Yakob proceeded to speak very fast, and in what sounded like perfect French. Armand smiled and shrugged, as if to say "It was nothing," and then Yakob said something to the owner of the café before turning back to Dez.

"We have to go now," he said, handing some money to the café owner as he brought a glass of wine to Armand. He smiled at the old man. "Thank you very much for looking after my nephew; it was very kind."

Dez went over and shook Armand by the hand. "*Merci beaucoup, Monsieur.*"

"It was a pleasure, young man." Armand showed the world all his brown teeth, his face creasing like old leather as he smiled. "I 'ope you 'ave a good rest of your *vacances*!"

"I'll try," replied Dez, thinking that, if they ever managed to get to their meeting point that evening, he'd have the most incredible "vacances" ever.

*   *   *

"How did you manage to get this?" Dez asked as he got into the passenger seat of the brand new Citroën ZX and reached for the seatbelt.

"I hired it."

"What with? You don't have any money!"

"I persuaded a machine outside a bank to give me some."

"Persuaded?" Dez gave the dashboard the once-over. After the one in *Stark Revenge* it looked like something off a Fisher Price toy, only not as colourful.

"The machine wasn't very intelligent." Yakob started the car. "There are smarter *plants* on Priam – it was easy."

"Why the new clothes? And where did you learn to speak French since you got off the bus?"

"I can learn very quickly by listening; it's something we are taught. By the time I left the bus I'd got most of it figured out." Yakob pulled out on to the road and accelerated. The automatic gearbox did the rest. "And I got the clothes to confuse anyone who might have been watching the bus. Did you see the car waiting this side of the town?"

"Yeah," said Dez, frowning. "How did you know they were Väds?"

"I had a feeling — I think you call it intuition — and even if I was wrong, which I don't think I was, being cautious never hurt anyone."

Dez fiddled around with the levers down the side of his seat and found the one that made it recline. He leant back. "Taking that money ... wasn't that like, *stealing*?"

"Theft?"

"Yeah."

"Only if it isn't replaced."

"You're going to pay the bank back?" Dez looked across at Yakob. "How? You've already spent loads of it."

"I won't do it personally." Yakob flicked his indicator on and passed a lorry loaded with metal barrels. "You know anything about computers?"

"A bit."

"Well, in a bank's computer money is just another piece of digital information."

"On and offs, zeroes and ones," interrupted Dez.

"Exactly. We can tap into any computer we want to here on Earth, so some 'on and offs' will be added to the bank's asset files. There'll be a bit of confusion as to where they came from, but everything will balance and no one will be out of pocket." Yakob tapped the steering wheel. "No theft, just borrowing."

Dez yawned. "*I* believe you, but thousands of policemen wouldn't!" He yawned again. "Lucky you didn't get caught."

"I suppose so. To change the subject, in the manner in which I have become accustomed to you doing, how did you find such a nice guardian as Monsieur Armand?"

"He was sitting at the back of the bus; didn't you notice?" Dez's eyes felt as if sand had been thrown in them. "Staying with him seemed more sensible than hanging around by myself out in the open."

"Good thinking, Dez."

They were both silent for a few minutes, and when Yakob next looked over at Dez he found that the boy was fast asleep, slumped in his seat with his mouth slightly open.

"Now *you're* on automatic," smiled Yakob. "Dream on, my friend, dream on."

The sun was making a slow dive for the horizon when Dez woke up. He stretched and yawned and then sat up with a jerk.

"How long have I been asleep?"

"Four hours. Nearer five, actually." Yakob pointed out of the window. "Have a look at where we are."

Dez brought the back of his seat up and saw they were high up in the mountains, travelling on one of those roads carved out of solid rock with a sheer drop to certain death on one side. This drop was on Dez's side.

He looked in awe at the black and white stripes flashing by on the low concrete wall that was the only thing between him and a final sky-dive, and was lost for words. High above the valley birds were flying parallel – *parallel!* – with the car ... right opposite him!

"Amazing view, eh?"

"I think I preferred it when I was asleep. Do you have to drive so close to the edge?"

"You scared of heights?" asked Yakob as the road swung round in a tight curve and started to climb even higher.

"Don't think so, but I've never been this high before."

Yakob indicated a map on the dashboard. "There should be a restaurant not far from here. Would you like some food?"

Dez dragged his eyes away from the view. "You bet!" he replied.

No more than five minutes later they were standing in the restaurant's car park, shivering from the cold.

"Let's get inside quick – I'm desperate for a pee!" said Dez, hopping about and rubbing his arms.

"After you, Desperate!" grinned Yakob,

bowing Dez towards the front door.

When Dez emerged from the toilet he found Yakob already seated at a window table, reading a newspaper.

"You should see the loos!"

"Why?"

"They haven't got any seats just, you know, footprints and a *hole*! Primitive or what?"

"Thanks for the warning." Yakob pushed a menu over towards Dez. "Take your pick, I'm paying!"

"The bank in Chambéry's paying," said Dez, opening the thick, leather-bound book. "It's all in French!"

"*Quelle surprise!*"

"Oh, very funny!" Dez closed the menu. "You order, clever clogs. Anything as long as it hasn't got mushrooms, broccoli or cauliflower in it."

Yakob raised his eyebrows.

"And it must have chips."

"Your wish is my command." Yakob looked around and waved at a waiter, who came straight to the table. "*Deux steaks, frites, un café et un Coca, s'il vous plaît.*"

"Steak and chips! My favourite!" said Dez, sitting back and rubbing his stomach.

"So you *do* speak French."

"Yeah, I'm fluent in food." He pointed at the paper. "What's in the news?"

"We are."

"We are? What d'you mean?" Dez leaned forward as Yakob folded the paper and turned the front page towards him. He saw a large, very fuzzy picture of something hovering in the air over some trees. A large headline below it screamed: *LES OVNI ARRIVENT!*

"Our little meeting with the Väd-Raatch didn't go totally unnoticed." Yakob took the paper back. "And the radio has been full of it all afternoon – I was listening while you were asleep. Apparently our flight paths took us up high enough for this country's defence forces to pick up on their ... what's it called?"

"Radar."

"That's it, radar." Yakob put the paper down.

"Who took the photograph?"

The waiter came over with their drinks, putting them on the table. "One very scared farmer, apparently," said Yakob when he'd gone.

"Doesn't look much like *Stark*."

"So-called military 'experts' are calling the picture a fake, and looking at it I don't blame them."

"Everything's all right then." Dez could see their waiter coming back with two plates loaded with food, chips piled high.

"Except that it seems, according to the radio, that everybody who owns a pair of binoculars is going to be out tonight watching the sky."

"So?" queried Dez as the plates were set in front of them.

"So we'll have to be even more careful."

"Mushrooms! You didn't ask for mushrooms, I heard you!"

"I've got them too, so they must come with the meal. Give yours to me."

Dez forked his mushrooms off his plate and on to Yakob's. "Why will we have to be more careful? No one's going to be looking way up here, are they?"

"Who knows? Maybe."

"Better safe than sorry?" asked Dez, cutting off a piece of steak, so soft it was like butter, and watching the juice spread across his plate.

"Much better," agreed Yakob. "It's the only way to make sure you live a long and happy life." He put his knife and fork down. "By the way, there was a small piece about your 'accident' as well; the police are mystified as to how it happened, but have listed all three of you as dead. I thought I should tell you."

The meat never got to Dez's mouth. "They think *I'm* dead as well?"

"Yes. The explosion left very little of anything, apparently."

Dez blinked and took a deep breath. He was past the point where crying about what had happened to his parents would help. He missed them, missed them badly, but nothing would ever bring them back and all he could do now was look forward. Surviving whatever came next was all he could think about.

"I'm dead." He looked down at his plate and sniffed.

"Do you feel all right?"

"I feel kind of empty," said Dez. "But I can't tell if that's because of what's happened or because I'm so hungry." He picked up his fork again. "I suppose there's only one way to find out..."

Chapter 10

It was pitch dark. The moon was hiding behind clouds and only the occasional star was visible through the gaps. Dez, who could still taste the ice-cream (with chocolate sauce) that he'd had for dessert, had given up trying to read the map by the light of the dashboard. The clock said it was 23.15.

Yakob drove very slowly with his headlights dipped. He was looking, he'd explained, for a small unmade track that would take them nearer to their rendezvous point with the scout ship.

"Are we on time?"

"We have forty-five minutes to get there."

He slowed down almost to a stop and swung the car hard right, off the smooth tarmac. "Here it is…"

All Dez could see was a space between the brush just wide enough to take the Citroën. The car bounced and heaved over the large rocks and stones that littered the rutted track. "You should've got a Land Rover," he told Yakob.

"I *should* be driving *Stark*, but I can't," replied Yakob, coaxing the vehicle carefully up the track. There was a muffled bang behind them.

"Whoops!"

"Whoops indeed. I hope that wasn't anything vital," said Yakob, stopping the car and listening.

"Maybe we should have a look. If something's wrong you'll never get back to *Stark* after you've dropped me off."

"Come on then." Yakob opened his door and got out. Dez did the same and found Yakob at the rear of the Citroën, shining his torch at one of the tyres. It was flat.

"Why did it do that?" Yakob asked.

"Must've hit a sharp stone or something."

"Isn't it self-inflating?"

"This is Earth, Yakob, not Priam IV," said Dez. "We'll have to change it."

"What for?"

"The spare. What else? Come on, it's in the boot." Dez popped the tailgate and reached in to lift up the carpet covering the spare wheel and jack.

"Have you done this before?"

"No, but I've watched my dad a few times." Dez took the torch off Yakob and began poking around in the well. "And if he could do it, it can't be *that* difficult – my mum always said he was useless at mending things."

"Will it take long?"

"Shouldn't. Why?" Dez found the jack and took it out.

"We still have to get to the meeting point."

"Well, don't just stand there – help me get the wheel out!" grinned Dez.

* * *

Because of the uneven track it had actually taken a lot longer than Dez thought it would to change the wheel, the whole process not helped one bit by Yakob's huffy complaining about archaic, ancient, antiquated and *awful* Earth technology.

It was now 23.40; only twenty minutes to go.

"Do you think we should park this thing here and hike the rest of the way?" Dez suggested.

"I thought you didn't like walking," said Yakob, steering the car gingerly round a bend.

"I don't, but I'm thinking of you."

"Very kind, and it's appreciated." Yakob fell silent, and for the next few minutes he concentrated on driving while Dez sat on the edge of his seat, watching their slow progress. "As soon as I find a place that's exactly what I'll do."

The road suddenly flattened out and Dez could see a place up ahead of them where the track widened slightly. Yakob pulled over and parked the car, turning the engine off, dousing the lights and sitting back with a sigh. In the silence Dez could hear the radiator fan whirring. When that stopped all that was left was the ticking of the engine as it cooled down. It sounded like an insect.

"Now we walk," said Yakob, reaching over into the back of the car and getting his haversack. "Ready?"

"Ready." Dez picked his bag up from between his feet and opened his door. The interior light came on and he saw Yakob smile.

"These machines aren't so stupid after all!"

"They've got computers in them now," Dez said, locking his door and closing it.

"Why give a tin box a brain?"

"*Stark*'s got a brain."

"It's a polymorphous hybrid transport unit; it needs one." Yakob looked at his wrist. "Come on, we haven't got far to go."

Fifteen minutes left.

* * *

Using the torch to guide them, they walked quickly in the cold night air, their breath blossoming out in front of them. They followed the track for some way and then Yakob pointed to a rocky slope and they scrambled up it, their hands and feet searching for holds, stones skittering down behind them as they climbed.

By the time they reached the top the track was some twenty or so metres below and Dez was out of breath and sweating from the effort. In front of him, in the beam of the torch, he could see they were on the edge of a wide, flat outcrop of rock, a wall of mountain rising up to their right.

"This it?" he wheezed.

"This is it."

"It's like a natural helicopter landing pad."

"It *is* a natural scout ship landing pad." Yakob swung the torch over to where the mountainside met the level rock. The beam found something that looked like a cave entrance. "Let's wait over there, out of sight."

"Just in case?" grinned Dez.

"As always."

It wasn't really a cave, merely a hollow in the rock. Huddled in it and wrapped in the heat-retaining sleeping bag, Dez felt safe and warm if not comfortable, but he'd lately come to realize that you couldn't have everything. He looked at his watch, pressing the button that lit the back up so you could see the time.

"Five minutes to twelve," he said.

"Five minutes to go, then. We made it."

"Just." Dez took a deep breath.

"They'll be here soon."

"Midnight on the dot?"

"That's the plan."

"That's what we call the Witching Hour, when the ghoulies and ghosties come out to play."

"You like monsters?" asked Yakob, shining the torch under his chin, like Dez had when the wild pigs had come sniffing round them.

"I like the *idea* of monsters ... I wouldn't want to actually meet one."

"With any luck you never will."

"What do you mean?" Dez frowned. "Monsters don't exist!"

"The Väd-Raatch do, and they're enough to make anyone's flesh crawl…" There was a high-pitched but soft beeping noise, like a phone ringing very far away. Yakob gave Dez the torch and reached into one of his pockets, bringing out a tiny box. A small red light on it was flickering. "Any moment now."

Dez looked out at the flat expanse of rock, grey against the black velvet curtain of sky. It was empty. Then the beeping stopped and became a single tone. Dez noticed that the red light had turned green, and as it did so it seemed as if all the air around them had been sucked away – he could almost hear a *FFFFF-WHPPP!* – and blown back again, like a giant taking a deep breath and then exhaling.

There was still nothing out on the small plateau.

"What was that?" Dez asked, wiping some

dust out of his eyes.

"That's called being on time."

"But there's nothing there!"

"Either you are very forgetful or you have an extremely short memory." Yakob pressed the box in his hand and an orange light joined the green one.

"What have I forgotten?"

"Cloaking."

"You mean the cruiser's arrived?" Dez squeezed the torch, sending a beam of light out on to the rock, and started to get up. Yakob reached out and pulled him back down again.

"Turn that off and don't move! You *must* stay here until I tell you to come out."

As he spoke there was a hiss of escaping air. Out in the middle of the landing spot a thin line of light, like three sides of a round-edged square, appeared in the night sky a metre and a half off the ground. It looked totally weird, so odd that at first Dez's brain couldn't make any sense of the information it was receiving from his eyes. Then the thin line of light got thicker and thicker and Dez could hear the whine of a motor.

"It's a door!" he whispered to himself.

"They've forgotten to turn the lights off!" muttered Yakob.

"Do they come on when you open the door of a scout ship as well?" said Dez, nudging Yakob, with his elbow. The light suddenly went out, but Dez could still hear the motor as it carried on opening.

"They must be nervous," commented Yakob, as the pitch of the motor changed.

"Not half as nervous as I am! What's happening now?"

"They're putting down the steps."

"Can you see anything?" said Dez, peering hard into the gloom.

"Not too much."

Then, as Dez's eyes got used to the dark, he could make out a patch of the night sky that wasn't so black. In it he thought he could see a figure moving. As he watched, the figure began to bob in mid-air. Dez squinted harder and then realized that whoever it was was walking down the steps to the ground.

When the shadowy figure had reached the ground (was that a gun he could see in his hand?) he heard a voice calling Yakob's name.

"Stay here."

"I'm not going anywhere, me," said Dez, watching Yakob get up and, running low across the flat rock, go to meet the waiting figure.

Dez strained to hear what they were saying, then remembered that even if he could he wouldn't be able to understand a word of it. He could see that Yakob was asking for something — something, from the way the other man was moving his hands, that he didn't have with him.

The next thing he knew, both men were walking back up the steps and into the scout ship. He was left completely alone, and even the sleeping bag wrapped round him couldn't stop the shivering. He huddled as far back against the rock as he could, scrunching himself up like a hedgehog.

He felt abandoned, exposed, at the mercy of whoever or whatever should choose to have a go at him. It reminded him of the time he'd been bullied at school and had had to spend almost the whole of playtime hiding so he wouldn't get beaten up. Hiding in some stinky corner, waiting for the bell, knowing that if they didn't get him before the bell went they'd do it to him on the way home. This was one memory he'd be happy to forget.

Dez blinked. He'd been staring fixedly at the grey square of sky since Yakob had disappeared into it. He peeked at his watch. The figures 00.05.45 peeked back and it took him a moment to work out what they meant. For some stupid reason he'd set his watch to the continental 24-hour clock before going on holiday, then discovered it was a pain trying to work out what the real time was, and *then* discovered that he'd forgotten how to turn the display back to normal.

He looked at the watch again. 00.06.05 … six minutes and five seconds past twelve. If he kept using the back–light at this rate, he thought, the battery would run out and he'd have no idea what the time was, continental or otherwise. Then he saw two figures appear in the grey square of the door and his fear took a hike to the back of his mind once more.

He wanted to wave, to get up and wave his hands and shout and run over and clap Yakob on the back. But he knew he mustn't. He'd been told to stay still, stay quiet and stay alive. He waited and watched.

The two figures (one must be Yakob, mustn't it?) came down the steps. He saw one of them gesture to the other to stay where he was and start to walk towards him. He'd only gone a few paces when Dez heard his name being called and saw the figure beckon to him.

"Coming!" he said, starting to unwrap the sleeping bag. But it was all tangled up with his feet and all he succeeded in doing was rolling over like a sack of potatoes. When he looked up he was facing away from Yakob, across to the right of the rocky plateau. There, hanging in the air, were the blacker than black shapes of the Väd craft that had attacked them the previous day. He opened his mouth to shout a warning, but nothing came out.

Chapter 11

Things began to happen, and they began to happen very fast.

Dez found his voice and yelled at Yakob to get down. The Tylurian standing by the steps to the scout ship crouched down and fired a stuttering pulse of bright white laser fire at the Väds, yelling something at Yakob as he hot-footed it back inside his ship.

As Yakob started to run towards him, Dez saw the ground between them erupt. A hail of explosive blasts sent shock waves through the rock and sharp *C-RAACKS!* echoed off the mountainside. It was like watching a shoot-'em-up vid game from *inside* the machine, except this was more real than real, and so fast-moving that there wasn't time to be scared.

As the air around him sucked and blew, like it had a few moments before, Dez saw Yakob dive for safety, the air above him shattering with a blast so loud he thought his eardrums had surely burst.

"Where's my bag?" Yakob yelled above the noise as he pushed Dez back into the tiny cave. "My bag!"

Dez fumbled and found it. "Here," he said, ducking as splinters of rock ricocheted around him. He watched as the flashing lights exploding in the air lit the scene, making every action jerky and puppet-like. He saw Yakob put something in the haversack and take a gun out. It looked small – too small to be of any use against what was being thrown at them. Still, better than nothing, he thought.

"We've got to move!" Yakob pushed Dez behind him, reaching round the lip of the cave and firing the lightweight hand–held laser in the direction of the Väds.

"Where?" Dez yelled back.

"Anywhere but here! Back down! Next time I fire, run, get over the edge and just slide!" Yakob took a deep breath, "*Go!*"

Dez went. Something told him that stopping to think might be the last thing he ever did – no matter that he was about to throw himself over a twenty-metre drop while alien craft used him for target practice.

He went into a slide, as if about to make a really ace football tackle, and felt himself start to roll down the rock face. Going down would be a heck of a lot faster than coming up had been! Something whistled past him as he dis–appeared over the edge, exploding some metres away, and he joined the cascade of rocks and stones in the stampede to be first to hit the track below.

Above him he could hear the *ZAP! ZAP! ZAP!* of Yakob's laser gun, then, as he reached the ground, a cry of pain. Turning round he looked up and saw the silhouette of a figure come tumbling over the edge. He began scrambling back as Yakob, feet and arms splayed out to slow himself, slid towards him.

"Yakob!" he yelled hoarsely. "Are you OK?" If Yakob was dead then his own chances of survival were going to be worse than nil.

The Tylurian came to a halt next to him. "Yes ... and no," he whispered, breathing heavily. "I'm alive, but they hit me."

"Where?"

"We don't have time for that; we've got to get further away." Yakob let himself slide the rest of the way to the track. Instead of making off left towards the car, he ran across the track and dived into the bushes on the other side.

"The car's *that* way!" hissed Dez, pointing even though Yakob's back was to him.

"Can't use it," grunted Yakob, forcing his way through the thick brush. "They'd pick us off in no time."

Dez didn't wait to argue. He scuttled across

the track, feeling as if there was a great big luminous bull's-eye on his back. Pushing his way into the brush he followed Yakob down the steep slope, thrusting branches out of his way with one hand and grabbing others to stop himself from falling.

The vegetation seemed to be attacking him from every side, thorns digging into him and tearing at his clothes. He didn't care because at least he was still alive, still hurting, gasping for air and still getting away. In front of him he could see and hear Yakob steam-rollering his way down the slope, and then stopping. Dez skidded to a halt, a branch thwacking him in the face.

"Ow!" He batted it away. "Why have we stopped?"

"I think something's about to happen." Yakob was taking deep, quick breaths and Dez could see him wince with pain as he dug his left hand into his trouser pocket and took out the little black box. The green light was still on.

"What?"

"Listen…" Yakob stood still, like a cat waiting to pounce on a mouse.

BA-DADDA-BOOOOM!

The air was split by a series of furious explosions and a fist of hot air punched them both in the face, making them reel and stagger backwards.

"We got them!" grinned Yakob. He held the box out so that Dez could see it properly. The green light blinked three times and then went out.

"That mean something?"

"It was the scout ship signing off." Yakob put the communicator away. "I wasn't sure they were still here, or had even survived. For all I knew the Väds could have got them – it was such chaos out there *anything* was possible."

"So the scout ship blew up the baddies … does that mean your lot will be back to get me?"

"I'm afraid not," sighed Yakob. "Not right now, anyway."

"Why?"

"There's a good chance they weren't the only Väd ships in the area. If they come back it could start all over again, and we can't risk that."

"I'm still stuck here then?"

"Yes, stuck here and stuck with me." Yakob picked up a branch and began to hack at the bushes. "We must get back to *Stark* immediately."

"Can't we get our breath back? I mean the Väds are gone, we should be OK now, shouldn't we?"

"We may be, but that performance back there should have this place crawling with people any moment now, wouldn't you say?"

As if in answer to Yakob's question a lone siren wail whooped from somewhere in the distance, setting off an eerie echoing reply.

"Police," said Dez.

"And that's just the start of it – every alien-spotter for a hundred kilometres around will be running for his car." Yakob slashed his way through the shoulder-high bushes with the branch. "This place will be crawling with them by dawn."

"They'll have plenty to look at." Dez ducked as a branch Yakob had pushed aside came whipping back at him. "Oi! Watch out!"

"Sorry," Yakob said over his shoulder as he pushed through the last of the thick brush and came out on to a sparsely wooded slope that led down to a small river. "How do you mean 'plenty to look at'?"

"Well, they weren't playing table tennis up there, were they? I mean, that was a *serious* firework display."

"Very serious. Come on, let's get into the trees; we don't want to be spotted."

"And the Väd gunships, or whatever you call them – they blew up, didn't they? There'll be loads of bits lying around – souvenirs." Dez followed Yakob, jogging down the slope.

"No, no souvenirs," replied Yakob, slowing

down once they were under cover of the trees. "The explosions were the result of vaporizer salvos. They'll be lucky to find dust."

"Could the Väds have done that to *Stark* when they were chasing us?"

"Could have and would have, if they'd got the chance."

"Blimey!" Dez trotted after Yakob in silence for a few minutes, his mind buzzing as he replayed the screamingly insane few minutes when his life had hung by a thread – for the second time in two days, he reminded himself. What on Earth would Tim and Cy think, if he ever got to tell them the story? He decided they'd think he was a few players short of a football team, so nothing new there.

It occurred to him, as he jogged along – breathing fine, head clear, not even sweating – that, oddly enough, he hadn't felt so good in ages. Maybe there was something to this exercise lark, or maybe, more likely, he was simply glad to be in one piece. Whichever it was he realized he was ridiculously happy to be jogging down an Alp at – he checked his watch – a quarter to one in the morning.

His dad would have been amazed – his son, sole heir to the Danby millions (ha-ha!) and dedicated couch potato, actually enjoying a run.

They stopped when they came to the river and both of them got down and scooped up handfuls of achingly cold, but delicious water.

"Never tastes like this out of a tap," Dez said, wiping his hands on his jeans and then his mouth on the back of a dryish hand.

"It's good; we have something similar on Priam." Yakob sat back on his heels, shaking drops of water off his fingers. "It always tastes better closest to the source."

"Is your arm still hurting?"

"My arm? No, not really." Yakob turned it to him to have a look and Dez could see a neat hole on either side of the sleeve. "A high-boost flux shot."

"What's that when it's at home?"

"A type of laser. Lucky really – if they'd hit

me with a deep resonator I'd probably have lost the arm."

"Why?" Dez moved round to have a closer look.

"Deep resonators make a tiny hole when they hit and then spread out in an arc. Very messy."

"No kidding!" Dez stood up. "Hasn't it left a hole in your arm?"

In reply Yakob rolled his sleeve up and showed Dez the two tiny scars, black against his pale skin. There was hardly anything to look at.

"Don't you bleed?" queried Dez, reaching out and touching Yakob's arm. "You're not a, like, *robot*, are you?" The skin felt quite normal, but then he was a person (a *creature*?) from a planet 300,000 light years away who drove an invisible van.

"No," replied Yakob, rolling his sleeve down. "I'm not a robot, but then I'm not human either."

Dez stood and looked at Yakob. The clouds had cleared a little and although it was still dark there was a pale light from the sky which made him look as if he was made from modelling clay. He'd known, almost from the moment they'd met, that Yakob was an alien, but he hadn't really had the time to think about what that meant. Too much had happened; there'd been too many close shaves and far too much excitement.

He was about to ask more questions when they heard the sound of a helicopter in the distance, the deep, rhythmic throbbing of its rotor blades becoming louder by the second.

"That's not the—"

"No, it's not the Väds," Yakob answered the unfinished question. "But we should move on, and keep out of sight. If we can put a bit more distance between us and this area, we can sleep till dawn and then make the nearest town for breakfast."

"How are we going to cross the river?" asked Dez. At the point where they were standing the river was actually more of a stream, only some two metres wide, but quite fast flowing. It could only get wider and deeper the further down they went.

"We won't need to." Yakob got up and stretched. "From what I remember of the map, this little thing meets up with a bigger one and we can follow that to where we want to go. Good, eh?"

"Triff!" said Dez. And then he remembered something, something he'd been meaning to ask Yakob. "Why did you go into the scout ship, back up there on the plateau? Looked like you were having an argument with the bloke who came out."

"I was."

"What about?" asked Dez, as they started to follow the river.

"He'd forgotten to bring the new cloaking device with him; it was still in the ship," Yakob shrugged as he walked. "He was nervous, I suppose."

"Not half as nervous as I was. I thought I'd never see you again – I thought I was going to die when the Väds appeared!"

"It was bad up there. We nearly lost everything. That spy is making life very difficult."

"Why can't they catch whoever it is?"

"They're too good, or too highly placed or, what is more likely, both."

"Why would a Tylurian want to help the Väds if the Väds want to kill Tylurians?" Dez's stomach rumbled. "Have we got any food left?"

"Money and yes," replied Yakob, stopping for a moment.

"What?"

"Back where I come from we have a saying which translates something like '*Money has no enemies*'." Yakob took off his haversack, opened a pouch pocket and dug around inside it.

"My gran, who was a bit odd, had a sign up in her kitchen that said 'Money is the Root of All Evil'." Dez accepted the silver-wrapped bar that Yakob gave him. "I dunno. I thought money was just money – stuff to buy stuff with."

"That's because you've never had large amounts of it."

Dez opened the foil package. "I've got £280 in my building society!" He bit into the bar. "Mmmm!" he said. "Crunchy, chewy and sweet – what are they called, Space Bars?"

Yakob watched Dez demolish his food while slowly opening his own bar. "No, it's called OPR, actually." He saw Dez frown, unable to talk because his mouth was crammed full. "Off-Planet Rations."

"Not very catchy."

"Filling though."

"Did you get the new cloaking device after all that?"

Yakob patted his backpack. "Safe and sound."

"Not a complete disaster then?"

"Not as long as we can get back to *Stark* in one piece."

As they made their way downriver it became obvious that there was an increasing amount of activity in the area. More and more sirens wailed, the sound of helicopters thrummed the air and the sky lit up with occasional flashes. The quiet alpine night was quiet no more.

But it was all happening further and further away as they jogged down the valley. Not for one moment did it occur to Dez that their escape had been too easy, and when the helicopter roared overhead he was so stunned that he stopped running and stood stock still, like a rabbit caught in a car's headlights, looking up to see where the noise was coming from.

Yakob ran back to get him, dragging him towards the trees as a spotlight lanced through the dark and started to sweep the ground around them, its incredibly bright white beam looking almost solid, almost touchable.

The combination of the noise, the buffeting wind and the probing light threw Dez's mind into a whirl. He couldn't think straight. Part of him knew that it wasn't the Väds, that it was just a helicopter, but part of him expected to be vaporized at any moment.

He flung himself on to the ground and scrambled behind a tree trunk. "Are they trying to kill us?" he yelled, in an effort to make himself heard above the din.

"I don't think so," Yakob yelled back, taking off his backpack and reaching inside it. "This is just their not very subtle way of trying to find out what happened."

Dez watched, open-mouthed, as Yakob took out his laser pistol. "Are you going to *shoot* them?"

"Not them, their light." He leant against the tree trunk for support and took aim, steadying his right wrist with his left hand and following the helicopter as it hovered in the air, swaying.

The spotlight swung around lazily, stopping here and there and making the shadows of what it found dance madly on the ground.

"Stay still, stay still!" muttered Yakob as he

sighted down the barrel, one eye closed. The beam turned and began to trace a path towards their hiding place. Yakob took a deep breath and held it. The beam crept nearer, wavering slightly as the person controlling it aimed it up the slope.

Dez, now also holding his breath, watched as Yakob pulled the trigger. The moment the spotlight was about to hit them the end of the laser pistol glowed and then the world went black. Still noisy, but black.

"Yes!" Dez punched the air and clapped Yakob on the shoulder. "What a star!"

Yakob grinned and moved back behind the tree. "My aim is true."

A thought struck Dez. "Won't they know someone's here now you've done that?"

"They'll think their equipment's failed and go back to base. I didn't blow the thing up, I simply burnt it out."

As if it had heard what he said, the helicopter rose up, banked and roared away, its tail–light flashing angrily.

"Will they send another one?"

"Can't tell – I've no idea why they were looking here in the first place."

"D'you know," said Dez, leaning back against the tree and scratching his scalp with both hands, "if nothing exciting *ever* happens to me *ever* again in my *whole* life I won't care. Honest." He looked up at Yakob, who was standing, listening. "Can we go somewhere and have a little kip? I'm trashed."

"Translate."

Dez yawned. "I'm tired."

"Me too, but we should go a little further maybe."

"OK, you're the boss." Dez got up and yawned again. "Let's hit the road, Yakob."

About an hour later, and nearly a kilometre farther on, Yakob called a halt for the night. It was nearly 2.30 in the morning and a cold wind had sprung up. Way back in the distance they could still hear and see evidence of the frantic searching that must have been going on around the site of the battle between the Tylurian scout ship and the Väd craft. Horns sounded, various airborne searchlights waved like magic wands and sometimes the wind brought them snatches of voices bellowing out of loudspeakers. Dez had a friend who lived near Wembley Stadium; he'd stayed there once when there'd been a rock concert and the effect was similar – without the music, of course.

They found somewhere out of the wind, unfolded their sleeping bags and got in, using their backpacks as pillows. It wasn't a bed, thought Dez, as he curled up in a ball, and it wasn't home, but who cares? At least he'd survived another day.

"Sleep well, Dez," said Yakob, patting him on the back.

"I will … and don't you worry."

"About what?"

"There aren't any wild pigs up here."

"Good."

"Just wild goats!" A pine cone bounced off

Dez's head, and he fell asleep with a grin on his face.

The airwaves almost hiss with poisonous conversation. In the world of the Väd-Raatch failure is a disease.

"What happened?"

"We don't know. Communication has ceased with the hunter units."

"Nothing?"

"Nothing."

"Have you sent reinforcements?"

"Too risky. There's an extremely high level of activity down there."

"Action is never too risky when the survival of our race is at stake."

"We will try."

"Trying is not good enough. Our target is just a boy, after all."

Chapter 12

When Dez woke up the sun was shining, and he could smell the vaguely familiar aroma of something hot and foody. He rolled on to his back, stretched and sat up, holding the sleeping bag up to his neck so as not to let any warm air out.

"Is that breakfast?" he asked, his eyes still closed.

"Best meal of the day."

Dez opened his eyes and saw Yakob sitting nearby, holding a steaming foil package in one hand and a bottle of juice in the other. "What's the time?"

"Time you got a watch."

"Ha-ha!" Still holding the sleeping bag tight with his right hand, Dez pushed his left hand out and squinted down at his watch. "6.30! I'm going back to bed!"

"Later," said Yakob, putting his juice down and picking up a map that was lying on the ground next to him. "We still have a way to go. The nearest place we can rent another car from is about eight or nine not very easy kilometres away. If we go fairly soon we might just get there by lunchtime."

Dez groaned, slumped in a heap on the ground and then started to crawl out of his bag on all fours. "This is worse than term-time."

He slouched over to the river and splashed some water in his face, the shock of the icy cold making him gasp. He stood and looked down at himself. His clothes were a mess, torn, dirty and crumpled, and his hands were filthy and covered in small cuts.

He glanced at Yakob. He looked no better. "How are we going to walk into some French town and rent a car looking like this? We'll get arrested!"

"We do look a bit like a couple of what we would call, um, roamers!" Yakob smiled as he stood up and looked down at himself.

"We call them tramps, and we look a *lot* like a couple of them!"

"Come and have your breakfast and we'll sort something out after that."

The sorting out ended up as a half-hearted attempt at dusting off and wiping down, at the end of which the two of them looked like a pair of slightly cleaner tramps. It would have to do.

It was close to 7.30 when they set off in the direction of somewhere called St Jean. On the map it looked as though it was downhill all the way, but the road maps supplied with hire cars can sometimes be a little less than truthful and there were plenty of small ups to go with the long downs.

As before, they kept off the roads, staying

with the river as much as possible and trying to keep out of sight of any cars. As they got closer to St Jean this became impossible and they decided that it would be all right – and much quicker – to join the road and finish their journey as if they were hikers.

They noticed that traffic was becoming quite heavy in the direction of the peak where they'd been the previous night. At the first shop they came to Yakob bought a couple of bars of chocolate and a newspaper and they sat by the side of the road and took a break.

"What does the paper say?" asked Dez, between mouthfuls.

"The headline says '*La guerre des étoiles!*' and there's a lot of utter nonsense about fleets of spaceships and nuclear explosions – these are stories for children!" Yakob put a piece of chocolate in his mouth and read on. "Oh!" he said, looking up and nodding his head. "*This* is good!"

"What is?"

"We have apparently been kidnapped by

163

aliens from – some 'expert' says – the Andromeda system. Ha!"

"Well, we were nearly killed by some aliens, so he wasn't so far off."

"True, but the *Andromeda* system! It's ridiculous!"

"Why?"

"Everyone knows there isn't a civilization in the Andromeda system that can split the atom, let alone master interstellar travel."

"Everyone on Priam IV might, but what do we know down here? Any pictures?"

Yakob flicked through the paper. "There are pictures of people trying to get up there." He held the paper open so Dez could see the photo of a traffic jam.

"Why do they think we've been captured by aliens then?"

"They found our car. Someone at that restaurant we stopped at spotted us driving off up the mountain." Yakob turned back a page. "It says, let me see... '*The mystery couple – thought to be father and son – were last seen leaving* Le Bon Goût *at about 10 o'clock, and their car, hired that day in Chambéry, was found abandoned near the site of last night's extraordinary incident. A white sun hat and a baseball cap were left in the car, but otherwise no sign has been found of them.'"*

"I've disappeared twice in two days – I think that must be something of a record." Dez popped the last piece of chocolate in his mouth and chewed. "I liked that cap as well. D'you think it'll be three days in a row when they find this next car dumped?"

"*If* we get another car." Yakob folded the newspaper and put it down. "I hope they haven't all been hired by idiots trying to get up the mountains."

"Let's go and find out, shall we?" Dez reached out and pulled Yakob up and they walked off towards the town.

As they came closer to the centre, more shops began to appear on the streets. Dez stopped outside one and looked at his reflection, and that of Yakob standing next to him.

"Do you have enough money to buy some new clothes?" he asked.

"Sure."

"*And* hire the car?"

"Yes."

"There's a sports shop two doors down." Dez pointed to a sign sticking out into the street. "I'm fed up with looking like a scarecrow."

Ten minutes later saw them both back out on the pavement dressed as if they were about to go to the sports track. And after a visit to a restaurant with a reasonable toilet, Dez for one felt a hundred times better than he had when he'd woken up that morning.

It was nearly lunchtime and the streets were almost deserted. They were walking up a steep hill, following the directions of the restaurant owner, when Yakob suddenly stopped and pulled Dez into a nearby doorway.

"Why'd you do that?"

"I think I just saw a Väd."

"What, *here*?"

"Shhh!" Yakob leaned forward slightly to look back up the street. "He's walking this way."

"What are you going to do?" whispered Dez. "Shoot him?"

"Can't. I may be wrong."

"Great." Dez turned to look at the door behind them. He reached out and turned the handle. Locked. Even greater. He turned to see what Yakob was doing and found he wasn't there. His mind froze; he couldn't think and for a moment he couldn't move. Where could he have gone?

Making an extraordinary effort he forced himself into action and peered out into the street. A few metres up the pavement he saw Yakob walking towards a man in a grey suit. He saw him stop and ask the man something. He saw the man look down at his wrist, and as he did so he saw Yakob's hand whip out, like a snake, and press the side of his neck. The man crumpled, slumping into his arms.

Dez sprang into action and ran up the street. "What are you *doing*?" he hissed.

"Checking," replied Yakob. "Help me get him back to the doorway."

"What if someone sees us?"

"We're just helping someone in trouble."

"*We're* the ones in trouble!"

"Not if we act calmly," said Yakob, dragging the limp body of the man back to the doorway. Dez took an arm and tried to help.

"How will you be able to tell?"

"Tell what?"

"If he's a Väd of course, what else?"

"There'll be signs," said Yakob mysteriously, pulling the man into the doorway and dumping him on to the ground.

Dez watched as the Tylurian began going through his pockets.

"Keep a watch on the street," said Yakob.

"OK," replied Dez, looking away. But he found himself glancing back at the slumped figure on the ground. He saw Yakob lifting the man's eyelids and closely examining his

168

dead-looking eyes. He let the lids drop and then reached into the man's jacket.

"I was right." Yakob stood up. He was holding a small, light grey gun. It looked as if it was made out of plastic. "A Vatrik-9. High-speed pneumatic."

"Not a toy, then?"

"Not unless you're playing for keeps," said Yakob putting it in his pocket. "Fires tiny explosive needles, hundreds per second."

"What are you going to do with him, the Väd?" Dez looked back out on to the street. "Kill him?"

"Not my style, and no need. He'll be out for at least a couple of hours, time enough for us to get away."

"What did you do to him?"

"Shut down his central cortex. He was careless, wasn't thinking and let me get too close to him."

"How did you know he wasn't just your ordinary Frenchman?" asked Dez. "He *looks* like anyone else."

"I recognized him from the other day. Remember the man standing by the car as we came into Chambéry?" Dez nodded. "Him," said Yakob, pointing at the man in the doorway.

"So there must be others here! What are we going to do?"

"Get to that car hire place as fast as possible."

"Let's go then," said Dez, giving the Väd one last glance. "What'll happen to him?"

"He'll wake up with a killer headache and won't remember a thing."

Back on the street the two of them hurried on up the hill and turned right into the road the restaurant owner had told them about. Some two hundred metres away they saw the sign for the car hire firm.

"What are we going to get this time?" said Dez, as they opened the door to the office and walked in.

"Anything they've got."

To Dez's delight the owner told them he'd

just had a Suzuki Vitara returned that morning. It was checked and ready to go. Dez took off his backpack and sat on a chair by the counter. As they waited for the man to fill in some papers in the back office a policeman walked in and approached the counter. He looked at them both and Dez, who wore guilt like a neon sign, immediately got up and went over to examine the car tyre pressure chart closely.

He didn't know why he felt guilty. Neither he nor Yakob had done anything wrong – except "borrow" some money from a bank's machine. But then, he thought, maybe someone had seen them with the Väd and told the police they were a pair of muggers. As he looked at the blur of type in front of him he supposed he could be feeling guilty because it seemed as if he was on the run, not just from the Väds, but from the whole world. The policeman started talking to Yakob.

Dez strained to understand what was being said, but his French simply wasn't good enough to make out anything but the occasional word. He cursed himself for not paying more attention in class, and vowed that, should he live to ever do French again, he would be all ears all the time.

The policeman sounded as if he was giving orders, but policemen everywhere always seemed to sound like that. Dez didn't dare say anything; he didn't even dare turn round in case the policeman noticed him and started asking him questions. He was going cross-eyed staring at the chart, so he moved along a bit and found himself looking at a large map of Europe.

He stood back a pace and looked up and over to the left hand side. There was England (or was it Britain? he could never remember), all green and tiny and floating off the coast of France. Would he ever get to see it again, or would this rotten secret code they'd stuck in his rotten DNA put the kybosh on that? Lost in thought he jumped a mile when a hand tapped him on the shoulder. He turned, half expecting to see Yakob in handcuffs and the policeman pointing a gun at him.

It was Yakob, without handcuffs. "The car's waiting for us round the back," he said.

"Great!" Dez turned and made for the door. Yakob joined him outside and they went looking for the entrance to the garage where the Suzuki was parked. "What did that *gendarme* want?"

"Nothing really."

"He sounded as if he was telling you off or something."

"He was telling me that it would be inadvisable to take a certain route up the mountains today because there are roadblocks everywhere. I told him we were going in quite the opposite direction."

Dez was about to reply when he heard a shout.

"*Attendez!*"

He looked back and saw the policeman holding something in one hand and beckoning them back with the other. "What does he want?" All his panic, guilt and fear came flooding back and he felt like haring off as fast as he could.

"It's your backpack," said Yakob, putting a hand on Dez's shoulder as if he knew what he was thinking. "You left it in the office."

They drove out of St Jean and followed the signs for Lyon, making sure they didn't go through Chambéry. It wasn't just the thought of the spooky Väd lookouts that made the longer trip worthwhile; Yakob didn't want to risk being recognized by anyone, especially the man he'd rented the Citroën from. As far as either of them could tell, they weren't spotted or followed by anyone.

"Have we been visited by aliens for a long time?" asked Dez, chewing on some gum to help his popping ears.

"As far as I know *we* came here first around the time you were born. I don't recall ever doing a class on this system at school, but someone must've known about this planet to have picked it as a hiding place."

"There's always stories about UFOs and flying saucers, but no one's ever seen a real one and all the photos are like that one in the paper, all blurry."

"You've seen a couple – you've even flown in one."

"Me?" Dez looked up from fiddling with his Walkman. It was the one major casualty from the Battle of the Plateau.

"UFO stands for Unidentified Flying Object, doesn't it? I think *Stark* fits into that category very well, wouldn't you say?"

"Yeah. Trouble is, who'd ever believe me? I saw a programme once, on TV, where they interviewed people who said they'd been in flying saucers and they all looked like complete nutters." Dez fell silent for a moment. "I haven't gone mad, have I? I mean, this *is* all real, isn't it?"

"Afraid so, Dez."

"So I'm not going to wake up in my bed and find it's all been a terrible dream, like in the movies?"

"This is about as real as it gets."

"I had a feeling it was." Dez put the Walkman back in his bum-bag. "I've got a good imagination, but even *I* couldn't have dreamed up the Väd-Raatch."

They drove on, passing through Grenoble, stopping outside the city for some lunch and then carrying on, joining the road where they'd caught the bus to Chambéry. That all seemed so long ago, so far away, the memory of the bus ride and of meeting Armand overlaid by more recent and truly bizarre events.

Dez had been so deep in thought that when Yakob turned the Suzuki off the main road and on to a small track he was disorientated for a moment.

"Where are we?"

"Not far from where we left *Stark*, about half an hour's walk."

"Only half an hour?" Dez undid his seatbelt as Yakob parked the Suzuki out of sight. "That's hardly a walk at all!"

"Well, *there's* a change of attitude," grinned

Yakob, switching off the engine and reaching for his haversack. "When I first met you the thought of half an hour's walk caused something of an uproar."

"I've changed," said Dez getting out and closing the door. "Being a dead person does that to you."

"It's true, you have changed." Yakob joined Dez and they started walking. "You are an amazing person, Dez."

"I'm not amazing; why should *I* be amazing? You're the amazing one, with your laser guns and cloaking devices and not bleeding when you're shot."

"That's just who I am and the job I do, I can't help it." Yakob turned and walked backwards as he spoke to Dez. "You have had to deal with some terrible things in the last few days and you've come through it all with your sense of humour intact; you've been scared, and you don't mind admitting it, and you have the wisdom to know that the only thing you can do now is look to what the future holds. I hope I could be like you if I was in your position."

"Watch out!" Dez pointed behind Yakob, but it was too late, he'd already stepped in a large, fresh cowpat in the middle of the track. Dez stifled a laugh. "Glad I'm not in *your* position now!"

"What *is* that?" Yakob asked, wiping his foot on some grass.

"You don't want to know."

"I do."

"It's called a country pancake," Dez grinned mischievously. "Cows don't use toilets, they just dooflop wherever they like. Don't you have animals on Priam?"

"We have lots, but none of them produce anything as vile as this!"

The rest of their walk was quite uneventful and Yakob, using his little black box, guided them through the forest towards the clearing where *Stark* lay waiting for them. There was now a circle of green lights on the box, and as long as they followed the direction of the one that pulsed they would find the van with no trouble at all, according to Yakob.

They saw no hunters and little evidence of anything a hunter would have been interested in; the odd squirrel and the squawk and flutter of a disturbed bird were the only things that proved the forest hadn't been abandoned.

Yakob stopped. "We're close, about a hundred metres."

"Which way?"

"Over there." Yakob pointed through some trees, and Dez could just about make out a clearing.

When they were at the edge of the clearing, Yakob pressed the box. It beeped and Dez could hear an answer from the invisible *Stark*. He looked at where he knew the van was and was amazed to see a bird walking about, suspended in mid-air.

"Look," he nudged Yakob. "Magic!"

"Look," replied Yakob, pressing the box again and uncloaking the van. "More magic."

The bird, frightened either by their arrival

or by the sudden appearance of something very solid underneath it, flew off. They walked over, and Yakob was just about to unlock the van when the air above them was split by an almighty roar.

"What was that?" shouted Dez as the sound reached a peak and then began to die away.

Yakob quickly opened *Stark*'s door and got in. Dez followed and watched as he sat down in front of a console.

"Well?"

"*Stark*'s checking," said Yakob, his fingers racing over the bumpy surfaces in front of him as screens lit up and holo-displays threw pictures out at him. "Low-level jet overflight. Must be the military still searching for flying saucers."

The ringing in Dez's ears had begun to fade when he heard another sound, the sucking *WHUPP-WHUPP-WHUPP!* of a helicopter. "Is that one of theirs?"

"Theirs?"

"The Väds."

"No, no it's not," said Yakob. "And it's going off in the opposite direction as well."

"We're safe?"

"We're safe."

"Thank goodness!" Dez sat down. He couldn't believe the relief, the sheer pleasure of sinking into *Stark*'s soft, friendly, welcoming seats. He revelled in the comfort, tilting his seat and lying back as Yakob disappeared into the front of the van. The jets and the helicopter had almost been one scare too many.

"How are we going to get out of here without being seen?" Dez called out.

Yakob came back up, holding something small and gold-coloured in his hand. "We are now fully operational. We can fly and no one can see us!"

"What's that?" Dez sat up and pointed at the thing in Yakob's hand.

"The old cloaking circuit."

"*That* tiny thing?"

"That indeed."

"What are we going to do now? I mean now

that you haven't been able to deliver me to the scout ship."

Yakob sat down. "The plan was, remember, for me to go off and find the other two parts of the jigsaw puzzle. Get the second and third people with the altered DNA off-planet as fast as possible and up to *Tyson's Grip*."

"And now?"

"Still the same, except I'll have an extra passenger."

"Is that going to be a problem?"

"It will be for you," said Yakob, putting the broken cloaking device down. "Every hour you spend here you're in danger. We're going to have to be extra careful."

Dez tilted his seat back up. "I feel as if I've got a deadly disease inside me, a horrible virus. I could die any moment from it, and there isn't any cure."

"There *is* a cure."

"What?"

"As soon as you reach Priam, and the code is read, you'll no longer be of any interest to the Väds. Instant cure."

"So, Doctor, how long do you think it will be before I can have the treatment?"

Yakob sighed. "That depends on how quickly I can find the other two."

"Where are they?"

Yakob was suddenly getting very busy, muttering to himself, or to *Stark*. It was hard to tell, and Dez realized he'd taken for granted the fact of Yakob talking to the van, but what – or possibly who – was he talking to? He'd ask later; now he wanted the answer to another, rather more important question.

"I said, where are they?" repeated Dez.

"Who?"

"The other two." Suddenly all the windows went dark, although the light inside the van remained the same, just like day. "What's happening?"

"Nothing, nothing," said Yakob. "The others, yes ... well, one is in Africa, somewhere called Lagos, and the other is in America – New York, the place is called."

"Where are we going first?"

Yakob looked at a map that had appeared on the darkened windscreen. "Africa. It's nearest."

"And who's there? What's their name?"

"I only have the first two initials, and the general area where they live." Yakob consulted a small screen covered in Tylurian script. "BK. Their initials are BK, and I have to find this person with no help at all."

Dez looked round at *Stark*. Its lights flashed and pulsated, the displays were displaying like crazy and the whole place hummed with artificial intelligence. It occurred to him that it could hardly be called "no help at all".

"Can I get a drink?" he asked, getting up.

"Sure, I'll get you a cup," said Yakob, joining Dez in the back of the van. "What would you like?"

"Anything."

"Mezz?"

"Some of that juice?" Dez looked at the black circle on the console where he'd watched

Tor Kobal's holo-vid. "You got any more of those vids I can watch?"

"I've got a couple of games." Yakob gave Dez a cup. "Want to watch one now?"

"Thought I'd wait till we took off – sort of like an in-flight movie," he said, sipping some juice. "When are we leaving?"

"We left a few minutes ago."

Dez grabbed the edge of the console, even though nothing had happened. "We're *flying*?"

"We're nearly there," grinned Yakob.

Somewhere in the unending vastness of space a transmission circuit opens.

"You have something to report?"

"We've picked up a trace. Someone's on the move."

"Follow them."

The circuit closes. For now.